Praise for Chinese Letter

"Svetislav Basara—enfant terrible of Serbian contemporary prose—has written a heartfelt narrative about the age we live in."

—Tihomir Brajović

"Svetislav Basara has written a fragmentary book in which, despite lots of digressions, the central theme can be clearly seen—an uninterrupted dispute between, not quasi-philosophical, but quite existential terms of *I* and *Nothing.* Coming face to face with the wild emptiness in the world with no firm grounding is the characteristic of a whole trend in modern art—speaking 'about nothing' in a most convincing way, he writes about the status of individuality in this century."

—Mihajlo Pantić

Chinese Letter

Svetislav Basara

Translation by Ana Lučić

Dalkey Archive Press
Normal · London

Originally published in Serbian as *Kinesko Pismo* by Vidici, 1984

First English edition, 2004

Library of Congress Cataloging-in-Publication Data available
ISBN: 1-56478-374-X

Partially funded by a grant from the Illinois Arts Council, a state agency.

Dalkey Archive Press is a nonprofit organization located at Milner Library (Illinois State University) and distributed in the UK by Turnaround Publisher Services Ltd. (London).

www.centerforbookculture.org

Printed on permanent/durable acid-free paper and bound in the United States of America.

Chinese Letter

I

My name is Fritz. Yesterday I had a different name. Today my name is Fritz. I have nothing to say: I'm sitting in my room trying to type a hundred pages or so of my story. It seems nothing is happening. Yet, that's not true. Lots of things are going on: my heart is beating, my blood is circulating, my kidneys are somehow managing to purify my blood, the Earth is rotating (it almost makes me feel dizzy), and night is falling. There is some kind of incessant ticking in my head. My face is pulled over my skull; I have no idea what it looks like today, I just know that soon—if this ticking in my head doesn't stop—my face will collapse, like a crumpled plastic bag, and I'll go insane. This ticking feels like Morse code. I must be picking up the frequency of some radio station. I'll go insane if the ticking doesn't stop. I have a sense that I've become too big for myself: I feel as if I'm much smaller inside than the actual size of my body. I've just started writing, and already I have nothing to say. That's why I invent. But this isn't important: I was told to turn in about hundred double-spaced pages and so I'll type until I'm finished. Nobody told me what I should write about. But they gave me a deadline. They said: "We'll come back soon." That was a long time ago, and look how little I've written. And what if I die, if I don't finish my story? Let's *call* it a story. Perhaps I'm already dead? No. The dead don't speak. I certainly know very little about myself, yet I know that I'm not dead. Perhaps I'll never die. That's not impossible: time goes by very slowly. Life goes much faster. I'm talking too much about myself. I better talk about something else. If this "else" exists. I'm not sure that I mentioned that time passes more slowly in the apartment building where I live than in other buildings. The tenant's association decided so. Therefore, what I am writing right now, I am still not writing. At best I'm writing the second or the third sentence of the introduction. And in the meantime so many things have happened: three-hundred-and-sixty heartbeats, about a hundred ticks in my head, the Earth has turned about a tenth of a degree. If that's the best way of describing such things. How's this possible? It looks like I'm pausing for a long time between some of the sentences. That seems to be what I'm doing.

***

How did this all start? I haven't started from the beginning. It looks like I don't know what's going on around me. Yesterday everything was different. I had some personal belongings: a book and some letters. I don't have them anymore. I only have illnesses. Actually—I have more of a memory of illnesses because I'm not in any pain right now. I have no doubt that illnesses are still working to destroy me but I don't feel anything. I haven't read the letters. It's a pity. I might have found out something more about myself. At least my address. But I regret most . . . I wanted to say: what I regret most is the book. I hadn't read the last few chapters. I never would've read them anyway.

***

Yesterday I had a hard time. I was going somewhere, I took the letters and the book with me, and I was walking around thinking how nice it would be if I didn't exist and at that moment somebody slapped me on the shoulder and shouted: "Well, well, well, look who's here!" At that very moment my pleasant daydreaming about non-existence dropped like a rock into a pool of water, creating a series of concentric circles—little waves that physics teachers use to illustrate how sound spreads through the air. I turned around and saw a very tall guy. I didn't know him. It was obvious that the man had made a mistake. He kept apologizing, he thought I was a friend of his, but I was not that friend. The day started off badly. I was going to visit a friend of mine. He had been lying in a hospital for months now and it was about time I paid him a visit. Everything that was happening seemed very suspicious.

First of all, what kind of friend was he that, when I saw him in the hospital, it was the first time I ever saw him, yes, the first time in my life—this is what my friends are like. I sat down by his bed. Soldiers kept walking through the hospital room in camouflaged uniforms. Their barracks were somewhere nearby and I guess they were coming back from their duties. It might even be that they were coming back from war. It's possible: sprawled on a bed next to my (let's say) friend, there was a guy in a military shirt with a nasty wound in the chest. A hopeless case. And my friend was a hopeless case. And I was a hopeless case. And everyone, I now know, is a hopeless case. But I didn't know this yesterday.

***

The doctors were making all possible efforts to cure my friend so that he could die a healthy man. By the way: my father, on his death bed, used to say that for an honest man the best thing that can happen is to die healthy, surrounded by his family. Very idyllic, indeed. But, to make things even more confusing, the doctors themselves were hopeless cases. When things go wrong, nothing can stop them: that same day, at the same time, my friend was visited by his mother. But it was not his mother. I knew that because my friend was not paying any attention to her. I was sure she was somebody else's mother. Or at least a stepmother. My poor friend. He must have felt awful. He had a visit from a friend who is not his friend, and from a mother who is not his mother. Perhaps he was not he. I don't know how to explain this logically. I hate logic but sometimes I use it so that I won't die from anxiety. But even logic can't explain this: in the corner, on a bed without a bedspread, there was a marble statue of Julius Caesar. The passage of time had destroyed his nose, both ears, and left underarm. His skin was covered with a gray film and was cracking. (*Sic transit gloria mundi*!) Against all hospital rules there was a fresco of a woman on another bed—Simonida—with a blindfold across her eyes. I said to her kindly: "They gouged out your eyes, you pretty picture." She responded angrily: "Go to hell!" My friend's mother, who wasn't his real mother, said: "There, you see what children are like nowadays." I wanted to leave, but it wasn't easy to do so anymore: the doctor wouldn't let me.

***

"You have 3,300,000 red and 19,000 white blood cells," the white mask bending over my face was telling me. Your blood test looks bad. The infection has gotten worse. An operation is the only choice we have." I was afraid of the operation. I didn't have any trust in a hospital where lost cases were treating other lost cases, even the ones who've been dead for a hundred years. I wanted to treat the infection with antibiotics, but the white mask was adamant: the operation was the only choice I had. I signed my consent form for the treatment and I don't know what happened to me after that. Perhaps I had an operation, perhaps I didn't have an operation, I might have died during the operation, I might not have died. If I had an operation it might have been only for my appendix. I already had every other operation. I was really afraid of appendix vermiformis. The infection could have easily caused an inflammation. In that case I would have to have an operation. What if the surgeon who was on duty that day happened to have a female acquaintance who was the relative of an idiot who lived in the same building in which an unimportant artist I couldn't stand also lived? What if the painter somehow found out that I couldn't stand him, and told the idiot that I hated him? Rumors spread very fast. The idiot might have said to his neighbor that I intended to kill the sculptor; the neighbor would sooner or later tell her relative that I killed the architect, and the relative—since she was the surgeon's cousin—would tell the surgeon all this in strictest confidence. Surgeons don't like killers of architects. What if that day that same surgeon was on duty? What if he left several pieces of gauze in my head *by accident*. If things took that turn, and who can tell that they didn't, my head is probably festering. Then it would be quite easy to cut my head off. For antiseptic reasons, let's say. Yes, yes, the ticks in my head. Perhaps they put somebody else inside me. Medicine can do wonders. And to complicate things further: dead or alive (as they say on wanted posters) I finally made it out of the hospital. Quite legally, I suppose. Nobody fired a gun at me. And my letters and my book were nowhere to be found. All right, I thought, letters come every day. Others will come. Even if I died, the letters would still come. Letters keep coming for a period of time after somebody dies. But the book? What happened to the book?

***

What could have happened to the book? I was thinking about that for about fifty meters, and then I couldn't walk any further. I had a wall in front of me. That's all I can say about the wall. My condition at that time could be described as: *it didn't matter that I stood in the rain*, but this isn't what I wanted to say. I just want to try to remember the last sixty seconds and the last fifty meters: I take a step forward, then I shift the weight of my body to my left leg and then I step to the right. We usually don't think about the mechanism of walking, but when you start thinking about it, the complexity of this mechanism hits you in the face and you are simply unable to take another step. I did this thirty times. Times two. Went to the wall. I could have done this differently. But I didn't. I looked stupid staring at the wall. I don't know how long I stayed in this position. I don't know how I got back home. It's really difficult to explain some things. So, I made my way back home and tried to think about everything. But it wasn't working. I'm trying even now. But it's not working. Still, something has passed. Five minutes have passed, for example. Finally, some more time has passed. That's because I'm thinking about the events from the past. It takes time for time to pass. I remember that I was overcome by enormous fear. I was afraid that my mother or sister or somebody else could walk into my room and ask me where I was. And as it usually happens, somebody (I won't say who it was) walked into my room and asked me where I'd been. I didn't know what to say. I forgot the script. I should have said that I had an operation.

***

An hour or two later, the two guys came. They said abruptly: "Write!" I asked, "What?" "Whatever you want." "How many pages?" "About a hundred!" Going away one of them paused at the door:

"We'll come back soon," he said.

II

Today my name is Fritz again. I have one problem: I exist. My biggest success in life is that I'm not dead yet. My biggest failure in life is exactly the same thing: I'm not dead yet. I was born and as a result I suffer all the consequences. If I exist, that's because I wanted to. I don't see any other possibility. I honestly envy those who don't exist. Those with no names and shape. Those who have no clue that they don't exist. But sooner or later they'll be drawn into the game too. Everybody succumbs in the end. If it weren't so, people would stop having children.

***

Existence itself isn't a big problem. The worst thing is my doubt about this existence. It often happens that I have gloomy thoughts and then I wonder: don't I exist only when this somehow fits my surroundings; isn't this the very reason that my name is on different lists and records? Am I not living on a street named after a person, and in a house with a number on it, so that these indicators would make it easier for other creatures to find my whereabouts? Let's not fool ourselves: the names of the streets aren't there to honor the dead but to track down the living. Once you've been born, they simply *force* you to live. To the degree they want, when the circumstances are convenient for them. You see, I'm persecuted: they force me to write. That's an old trick: everybody writes about persecution. But I have nothing against this state of affairs. It even pleases me. If they didn't persecute me, I'd be in a vacuum, left with nothingness and—what's worst—left with myself.

***

I've been thinking a little bit about what I see and feel and it all seems very suspicious. When I say this, I am thinking of myself and my surroundings. What gave me reason to be suspicious? Nothing! Simply nothing. These are the rules of the game: they persecute me so that they can convince me that I exist. I wish I could trust them. I insist on being persecuted. My retreat from the world should result in their asking: Where the hell is Fritz? They should start looking for me, and when they find me they should persecute me. Thank God, they found me. They ordered me to write. Perhaps they want my statement. All right! This is a part of my statement.

***

"The postman brought a letter for you," my mother says. A blue, official, registered letter that reads:

Note: the following mathematical problem should be solved.

If a traveler goes from place A to place B, and if the distance between A and B is 86 km, and if he walks 5 km/h on average, how long will it take the traveler to get from place A to place B?

And, instead of a signature:

We'll come back soon!

***

That's just what I needed. Perhaps they know that I'm bad at math, so they want to make my job even harder. Where was I? Oh, yes. I have become submissive in my desire to be persecuted. For example, when in my rare walks I come across a policeman, I can hardly restrain myself from going up to him and saying: "I surrender! My name is Fritz! It's impossible that I'm not guilty. Take me with you!" However, I have never done this. Partly because of my cowardice, partly because of my *angular* way of looking at things. *Angularity*—that's my philosophy. I'm trying to observe all things by looking at them askance. The majority of people (those who see things at a 90° degree angle) see them as they are trying to appear. That's my view of looking at things when I'm crossing the street. This view is the safest in traffic. But life isn't made up of crossing busy streets, is it? Sometimes, you should look at things from an angular point of view. With this view you can't see anything except the misfortunes ahead. In spite of everything, I can't help but see things from an angular point of view, not even taking a peep at what's happening backstage, where you might see the destructive mechanism of deception. Let's take madness as an example. If somebody says that he's Alexander the Great, he'll be put into an insane asylum very soon. People have no problem with that. But there are lots of problems with doing this. I call myself by a different name each day; these days I call myself Fritz, and nobody says a word to me, nobody even thinks that I might be crazy. It's because Fritz is completely unimportant. But it's different with powerful people. The name Alexander the Great is important enough to instill fear in quiet, ordinary citizens and they do whatever is necessary to twist his noble plans, to intercept his visionary conquests that might crush their fragile—you could even call it "manufactured"—peace.

***

Or this: A friend of mine goes out for a walk, wanders out of town, walks into a field, and suddenly sees a dead lizard with ants crawling all over it. My friend stops and starts thinking: "There, only yesterday this lizard was running around freely, and now he's dead and the ants are eating him. Tomorrow comes, and hundreds of these ants will also be dead, squashed by the feet of passersby. Does this make any sense?" My friend keeps looking at this for about five or six minutes, tortured by unpleasant thoughts, and then he starts going back. On his way back, he forgets all about this, his mood improves, he comes to town, steps on the street and pop!—he gets hit by a truck. If he hadn't stopped by the lizard, nothing would have happened to him. As it is, he got hit by the truck. Broke his ribs, arms, pelvis, jaw, and so on. And my friend was taken to the hospital. That's where the complications began. One thing starts festering and then another. And there you see, my friend has been lying in the hospital for years neither dead nor alive and nobody visits him.

***

I hope they'll be satisfied. I've said everything I know about my friend's accident. I don't think there's anything more I can clarify. At first, when they told me "write," I thought this would be a kind of a game. Just a hundred pages. Now, all these unwritten pages frighten me. A hundred pages. I can hardly imagine. I don't usually think in terms of this amount. For instance, I'll never turn one hundred. I'll die before that. Besides, I don't write everything I intend to write. Word by word, sentence by sentence (there it goes, slowly) and suddenly there is a huge pile of impossible sentences fighting with each other, expressing something quite the opposite of what I want to say. While the sentence is in my thoughts, in my head, it is living and whole, but immediately after I write it down, it becomes a corpse and starts falling apart in front of my eyes, in words, syllables, then letters and in the end there is nothing left of the sentence but the ants that have chewed it. That's why I write and never look back. I have to type and type until the ribbon breaks, until the paper runs out, until I finish, until I die, until something happens. If I turn around to look, I'll become a pillar of salt. That's how it seems to me. I think I can scientifically prove this: I who started writing this do not exist anymore, and the I who will put a ● at the end of this sentence still does not exist. Only at this moment does this *I* exist. Now it doesn't exist anymore, because this is another sentence and some other *I* . . . Now I purposely didn't put a period at the end of this sentence but it doesn't help. I exist only momentarily. Generally speaking, this thing about my existence—it's all so uncertain. My hands start trembling when I think about it. I swallow a couple of Valiums and Xanaxes. Given the degree of my anxiety, these little tablets look ridiculous. Actually—they look sad. I almost feel sorry for these tiny, multicolored tablets that look much better than what they're capable of doing. They, I admit, do their best, they do all they can, but it's all in vain. Anxiety comes and goes as it will. Nothing can help here. Between certain chapters (let me use this word), hours and hours pass when I'm not able to do anything except walk around my room pressing my hands on my face. Anxiety has a dull, mongoloid face. When it appears, it horrifies me—not the horror of itself—but its inexpressibility. And what is there left of this world? What's happening to reality? The atoms are so tiny, they just pretend that they exist, and everything is made of atoms, which means that nothing is made of atoms. Mathematics, the foundation of all science, is based on an ideal conception of a dot and a straight line and on an insignificant amount of suspicious numbers. There is no logic in this. There's no room for me. And all this, including me, still exists although it doesn't exist. All I can do in my self-defense is look at the world *angularly*.

***

But no! They don't let me! My mother enters my room and tells me that my sister is getting married: "The family is here, everybody is happy and you're sitting here and writing some of your stupid things."

***

Getting married? So soon? She didn't tell me she was getting married. And when could she have told me this? I haven't talked to my sister for years now. I don't even know what she looks like. I almost forgot that I have a sister, and there she is getting married. Whatever, there is nothing I can do. The groom looks familiar for some reason. Oh, yes! That's the son of the butcher across the street. He has a mongoloid face. He looks like the sheep his father butchers. *Almost* like a sheep, of course. My sister has a similar face. You can't say that they don't make an excellent couple. Only today did I take a look at my sister's face. My God, she has changed so much.

***

"At this solemn moment I want to wish the two of you a long and happy life. My sister, it is your duty to love your husband and to respect him and to bear him children. You, my brother-in-law, you should protect your wife, and stay by her side in good times and in bad."

***

After I said this, I ran to the bathroom and vomited for a long time. But please note. In the bathroom, sitting on the washing machine, there was a woman in black. "Who are you?" I asked. (I don't remember seeing a woman in black among the invited guests.) "I am your widow," the woman said and burst into an awful scream. I hardly managed to flush the toilet.

***

Damn curiosity. My mother enters my room and asks me: "Who wrote to you?" I don't understand what she is trying to say. "That letter you received this morning." Oh, I see: "Nobody wrote to me!"

★★★

My mother is crying.

★★★

“Mom, why are you crying?”

★★★

It’s getting dark outside.

III

My name is Fritz again.

And I say:

– Mom, are you mad at me for what I said yesterday?

– No. I'm just worried about you. What is it that you've been writing for days now?

– I'm writing a statement.

– What kind of statement?

– I don't know. The two guys who came the other night, you remember, they ordered me to write. I have to write about a hundred pages. I guess this is a statement.

My mother starts crying, grabs her head, falls into despair and, pulling out strands of her hair, starts repeating like a broken record: "He has a statement to write, he has a statement to write, he has a statement to write . . ."

***

So:

Today I went to visit my friend. He works in the hospital's Department of Pathology. His job is to dissect, butcher, human corpses to try to find the cause of death. Deep inside me I think this is a useless job. All these corpses are dead enough, regardless of cause. I would like to say something more about the corpses in this autopsy room. The corpses lie on ceramic tables. They are all naked. First and last names are written on a piece of paper, tied with a strong thread to the big toe of their right legs. And some other details that I forget. And that's all. Otherwise, an impeccable order everywhere. Bottles with formaldehyde and organs standing next to one another as in a pharmacy. I have the impression that there is nothing more dead in this world than the corpse itself. A stone is full of life when compared to a corpse. This is my impression. Why do I keep going to the autopsy room? This isn't a difficult question to answer. My excuse is that I go to see my friend but this isn't very convincing. I can visit him at his home or invite him to my place. The possible reason: I go there to look more alive to myself by being surrounded by all those corpses. You can't find death there. Death has done its job in this place and went back to where it is needed, where life is. What do I think about in the autopsy room? About an absurd thing. I ask myself what I know about life. Nothing. I only know that it's unbearable for me and that—strangely—I'm very scared of the possibility that it might end.

***

We were sitting in the Department of Pathology and drinking coffee. Suddenly something caught my friend's attention. I looked at him curiously, and—with his face lit up—he said: "Look Fritz, what an excellent specimen of liver cancer."

***

I remembered one sentence that I wrote a long time ago. I will try to write it down again. Let it be known:

"The only thing I'm sure about is that she was leaving, she was leaving for a horribly long time, she enjoyed leaving, she left twice, thrice at the same time, she removed everything that could look like a coincidence and I have to admit—I've never met anyone who was leaving with so much skill, for such a long time, even longer than this sentence, and if she had been taking her leave for just a little bit longer, I think she would have left even before she actually came and then she was leaving, and leaving and leaving until she became a ● on the horizon, and after that even less than this and then hungry dogs would come by, finish what's left of the dot and die in horrible pain."

***

There is no use beating around the bush. I have to face an unpleasant fact. I will soon die. I don't know exactly when.

Perhaps in an hour, perhaps in a day, a month, a year, or thirty years. In any case, it all comes down to the adverb *soon*. If that's an adverb. Death is standing next to me, always ready, and I'm afraid. My life is nothing but a fear of death and finding the ways of making this fear less unbearable. And one more thing: my life is a constant digression from the subject. My job is not to die but to write. All right! I am writing! Actually I don't have a life. I pretend that I live. I'm putting lots of effort and time into this pretending, and it—sucking up my strength—is speeding up my already ever-closer end, but more or less I'm satisfied with the fruits of my effort, since the result of it is a solid illusion of life, so solid that I'm almost palpable. But here lies one contradiction: Life is quite simple, but also horrible, and it all comes down to the pumping of the heart, kidneys, liver, breathing and incessant repetition of unpleasant questions: how's all this possible? How did I come to be on this earth? What happens after death? I realize that I'm here only as a result of the function of the above-mentioned organs and to my asking the three questions, but I find it unbearable to always question myself about where I come from and to where I will disappear, because before and after death there is a great infinite unknown where there's not even the slightest trace of my *I*. I simply dare not think about the function of vital organs in order to avoid ruining everything. All around me there are cancers, cirrhosis, tuberculosis, bacteria.

Billions of bacteria. It's all a conspiracy to stop the functioning of my organs, to bring havoc into strained harmony.

And then—goodbye my fragile *I*, my inflated greatness, my unproven existence. From time to time I have a feeling that the whole universe is very fragile, and it takes so little for everything to turn into nothing. I took refuge in my room, inside my five or six walls. It's not much shelter. I built a fence around my hundred cubic meters of emptiness with thin walls made of even denser emptiness and this shelter of mine is actually my prison. Prison of my body that is a prison of my *I*. I can't move out of either cell. Nor do I dare. I'm fooling myself with some unfounded hopes. Actually, I'm making plans for some vague future. But I repeat: I will die sooner or later and there is nothing I can do to prevent this.

Except hang myself.

***

Just imagine this: she got married. Who would have expected this from her? Sisters just cause lots of trouble. Perhaps I didn't take good care of her. Now there is nothing I can do. I have to put up with them. And at night—it's clear what they're doing. And who would have thought she is so beautiful with that enchanting mole on her cheek, which slowly (but surely) is turning into melanosarcoma.

***

I felt melancholic.

I wanted to hear "Fascination."
I turned on the radio.
I heard "Fascination."
Then I turned off the radio.
I still felt melancholic.

***

And yesterday an unpleasant thing happened. I sat down to write; as usual, late at night; I felt just the average awfulness; nothing indicated that something unusual could happen, but an unusual thing did happen. Suddenly, I became aware that I *am not writing* sentences, but that the sentences are writing what they want and in a certain way they force me to write them down while making me feel as though I really want to write them down. As if I really had all these thoughts. I didn't dare read what I wrote in order to avoid being turned into a pillar of salt. I tried to resist. In vain. It felt as though I had fallen asleep in a boat in shallow waters, and woke up in the middle of a huge river. The sentences noticed my resistance and they raised their voices. (This scared me even more, and outraged the sentences.) They started yelling, screaming, scolding and this created an unbearable noise in my tiny little room, too small for even a couple of words uttered in a whisper. The noise woke up our neighbor. He got up, went down the stairs and started banging on our door. The banging came at an inconvenient moment. My hands were busy with tying the noose. I guess they wanted me to hang myself. There was nothing I could do. My hands threw the rope away and opened the door. The neighbor was standing there simmering with rage, wearing his pajamas and an idiotic nightcap. "Listen here!" he said in a voice of a quiet, ordinary citizen that I can't describe well. "It's three in the morning. I have to get up at five to go to work. If I oversleep and fail to go to work, everything will stop, my boss will be mad: he won't fire me—no, this won't happen (it would be my first time)—but he'll be mad, he'll yell, and I don't want that, do you understand that I don't want to get myself into trouble because you and your friends are having orgies all night long? Furthermore: my wife is very upset because of all this and she had to take a tranquilizer, which she could have made better use of some other time, because one can't find these pills in pharmacies anymore. My daughter is crying and she won't be able to concentrate on her exam tomorrow. If she fails, she'll fall behind her friends, everybody will make fun of her, and she might not even be able to get married to the right guy. What do you say to all this? How do you explain this?"

***

Suddenly I wanted to grab his neck and strangle him. All this is not particularly unpleasant, these things can happen, neighbors are constantly protesting because of noise, but something else is bothering me here. I'm not sure if I strangled my neighbor or not! I was sure he went upstairs to his apartment and that I didn't strangle him, but some time before dawn I became suspicious: "What if I did strangle him after all?" I didn't have an alibi. I had no evidence that I didn't strangle him. This is how things are with my paranoia. It works according to the principle of the NKVD secret police: Not possible I'm not guilty. If there is no guilt, my paranoia is there to find it. Well, all right! I admit (if and until proven otherwise): I strangled my neighbor, I put the corpse in a bag, and I threw the bag into the river.

***

It seems that I didn't strangle my neighbor after all. Several days passed by, I didn't go out anywhere, I was sitting fully dressed ready to surrender myself when they knocked on my door. If I had strangled him, they would have come to pick me up by now. But who can tell? Luckily, together with my paranoia I have a self-defense mechanism too. Even if I strangled the neighbor, I did it with diminished capacity. Anyway, sooner or later my neighbor would die. This is how my self-defense mechanism works.

***

I would have said in court: "So what? His daughter has been damaging my ears for years with her intolerable piano exercises."

***

"There's a letter for you," Mother said. A pink, private letter and it reads:

I have been watching you for years. I am unusually glad that you stood up to that idiotic father of mine. I am on your side. When I was a little girl you weren't different from all other tenants in our building. When the woman inside me awoke, more and more I began to see you as somebody that I would like to belong to. Of course, I did not show this in any way. It all came down to "good morning" and "good evening." I never said "hello," or "goodbye" to you. I hope you will find a way, you know what I mean. I am in deep trouble. Sometimes my spirit aspires to something sublime; I would like to exist as a meditative creature, but I am also a bitch. And I cannot find my way in this disharmony. When I am calm, I play music, read, think about eternity. It feels like I am flying. But very soon restlessness ensues and I have to go out. I fuck strangers that I meet by accident on the bench in the park. Or in a basement. Then I think: Mozart—that's stupid; music is stupid; everything is stupid. Afterwards I have terrible pangs of conscience. I am made of contrasts. Yesterday I strangled my poodle that I adored and for a while I felt great, like a master of life and death. Today I feel . . . I better not say anything about this. This is destroying me. Only you can end this nightmare.

Moira

***

God, how old can I be?

***

Now, I see. The neighbor's daughter has grown up already. Her name is Moira. She's eighteen. She's beautiful. She's been hanging around with people in the park. She plays the piano. She likes/does not like Mozart. She has green eyes. I love her.

***

Perhaps all this was just a dream. I wish all this was just a dream. I will retell it, I will mention it in my statement, I won't keep silent about anything. Perhaps all this is delirium tremens. I was drinking a lot in those days, I felt like 30% of me was made up of alcohol. I was thinking:

There is nothing that can shatter your reason, consciousness, fear, anxiety like CH_3CH_2OH. To get out of yourself: ethyl enables you to do just that. Your spirit goes someplace

and wanders around without noticing either itself or its surroundings,

and what remains is

a staggering and unsteady body.

And so

once

I found Moira's letter. Just three words, a question addressed to me:

Who am I?

And a similarly short answer:

You are nobody.

And then

what follows is the fantastic correspondence from which I discern that Moira is not quite herself. Description after description of the antique armoires lying on her during the night and strangling her with their weight; gray light hovering in her room for days and the pale Mozart spitting blood sitting at her BERNSTEIN (or something like that) piano.

"*Mozart is a ghost,*" writes Moira, "*but blood is not. It is real, foamy, bright red, steaming. Even if you wipe it off, the stains remain. My piano is like the face of a pimpled girl.*"

I am reading these letters

For a hundredth time, always starting from the beginning.

And I have a hard time making the decision. I take a typewriter, I go up to Moira's door (her father was at work), I put the typewriter on the concrete and I type lightly

knock, knock, knock . . .

But nothing happens. Behind the thick oak door the sounds of the piano are coming.

I go back to my room feeling ashamed

and watch the raindrops

coming down

<table>
<tr><td>c
o
m i
n
g</td><td>d
o
w
n</td></tr>
<tr><td>w
i
n
d
o
w</td><td>pa
n
e
s</td></tr>
</table>

However

I go up again. Perhaps she couldn't hear me

because of the music. I boldly press the bell

feeling anxious that this will make all the bells

in all the cathedrals go off, and that all my neighbors will come out to see me standing humiliated in front of the door. Still, what can be heard is only

a muffled buzzing. "It's open," somebody says

and I enter as if in a dream . . .

***

– Mom, where is the pink letter?

– What pink letter?

– The one that you brought me this morning.

– I didn't bring any letter this morning.

– Mom?

– Yes.

– Have you ever read Kafka?

***

I could swear I wasn't sleeping. I was writing. And what if I was dreaming that I was writing?

***

"Yes, yes, what if you only dreamt that you were writing?" My NKVD paranoia grins at me from the trash bin.

***

– Mom!

– Yes.

– Has my sister gotten married?

– Of course she has. What kind of question is that?

– And what's my sister's name?

– Stop fooling around.

– I'm not fooling around. I'm asking you.

– You're being silly. Her name is Anna.

– Mom, does Anna love her husband?

– Of course.

– Does he love her?

– What's the matter with you today? Of course he loves her.

– They love each other a lot?

– A lot.

– Mom!

– Yes.

– Have you ever read Stephen King?

***

I want to hear "Fascination."

I turn on the radio.

The news was on.

They say: "Mao Tse-tung died."

That makes me sad.

I change the station.

"This is the BBC. Mao Tse-tung died."

It makes me sad.

I turn off the radio.

You can hear the sounds of "Fascination" coming from somewhere.

***

So I have to go to Her and tell Her everything. She lives

in the attic. There's a small room upstairs behind a clutter of discarded things where She spends Her days sitting in a rickety rocking chair. I go up there secretly, make my way through the clutter, stand in front of the door and type silently on the typewriter (which is always with me):

knock, knock, knock . . .

Actually, She is not very much like a woman. She is somehow grammatically a woman because She's a female noun. There's no room for arguing with me about this. Her eyes are like two round attic windows, their color constantly changing. Sometimes they're transparently blue, sometimes gray, and every now and then a bird flies over Her pupils. When it rains, She cries. Her ribs are the ribs of an old radiator. Her breasts are two dusty lampshades, Her hands—torn pipes, Her legs—legs of a writing table . . .

and Her heart . . .

Her heart is the most important: It's an old Singer sewing machine. It sits comfortably in the breast of a rocking chair. It only takes starting the wheel and She comes alive, and her heart starts beating fast. Since it is old, it's not surprising that it suffers from various noises, tachycardias, and I would say angina pectoris . . .

I fear the worst . . .

***

"My dearest! Nothing works for me. I'm so alone, and nothing works for me."

IV

My God, what day is it today?
My God, what's my name today?

***

I woke up during the night. God, I thought, I was dreaming that I got a letter, and that I went to our neighbor's daughter, and then I was dreaming that I woke up and that I asked my mom what happened to the letter. The waves were splashing against my legs. That's the only thing I dreamt and then I woke up because I was cold. Still, one moment before I was fully awake, the waves really did splash my feet. I could see them clearly. Fear made me plunge deep inside myself and I tried concentrating on huge steel plates or marble blocks. The old trick. I thought it all out in advance but it didn't help. I was holding myself on the edge of the bed trying not to sink, but the bed started sinking too. Everything was sinking. In situations like this you should ask yourself some basic questions. I asked myself, Who am I? where am I? but I didn't get any answers. In a way I knew it was me, Fritz, but this *me* and the person, and where I was supposed to be, were also sinking and becoming somehow deeper; they weren't different but they were incomprehensible. There was no way out of it. I had to write everything down (the thing about my sinking) to stop getting away from the topic of my writing. I had to write so that I wouldn't die. Didn't they order me to write? I woke up during the night thinking that I'm not *here* but that I'm lying on a beach; I felt an unbearable emptiness within myself, the futility of everything around me; I sat on the edge of the bed and covered my face with my hands. The typewriter was sleeping. I woke her up so that we could write. There are no more Tranaxes or Xanaxes. Even if I had them, I doubt they could be of much help to me. Nothing happened that could disturb me; the sentences kept quiet yesterday; I was reasonably satisfied with myself, and now quite unexpectedly I'm sitting on the edge of the bed/madness, I'm covering up my face with my hands and I feel terrible. I have to write so that I won't die and I have to keep repeating this so that I don't forget. I know that starting a new sentence can bring relief, but I must not do that. The most important thing is that which remains behind me, at least superficially, a kind of continuity, something seemingly uninterrupted and something I shouldn't pay any attention to. If I pay attention, I will become IT; that is: nothing. Each new word and each new sentence brings hope that I'll say something that will bring my salvation, and that's why I'm writing as if writing brought me pleasure: quickly, breathlessly, determinedly; trying to have in front of me as many unspoken words as possible, as much hope as possible, hope which becomes despair the moment you write it down, but I keep on writing because I need hope, and you can find hope only in unwritten words and sentences. Just don't take any pauses. I have to write so that I won't die and I have to keep repeating this so that I won't forget. Writing won't get me anywhere (it's quite clear to me) but if I go back, I will *stay* there forever. For example in the sentence: "I am sitting on the edge of the bed/madness, I'm covering up my face with my hands and I feel terrible." No! I must not stop. But how can I go on? It's not difficult to say *I must not stop*. It's hard, it's almost impossible, to write. Cases, verbs, sequence of tenses, the whole of grammar, all this makes me even more desperate and sounds like I have to wear thick glasses, which only makes my already bad situation worse because I'm not shortsighted. Besides, lately I've been writing in a pretty strange style. First, I carefully sharpen my pencil, I prepare a stack of paper, think in detail about what I want to write and then, clenching my teeth I start poking my temple with the sharpened point of my pencil. By the time I write a single sentence, I'm completely exhausted. Blood keeps dripping on the paper while I'm retyping, the drops of blood are coagulating and stay fore●v●e●r between the w●o●r●d●s. By the time I write a sentence or two I'm completely exhausted. That's why I wear glasses. I'm writing all this so that I won't die and I keep repeating this so that I won't forget. I'm writing to keep my hands busy. I have two hands. I usually cover up my face with them, but sometimes I use them for other things too. For example, I use them for trembling. Writing is not their true purpose, but it's better for me if they write. This keeps them busy and this is how I can be pretty sure that the right hand won't cut the veins on the left one, or—which is even more dangerous—that they both won't strangle me. If I could, I would nail them to the table. But there is a problem here. I can nail one with the other. But what to do with the other one? Perhaps I can ask somebody to help me nail down the other one?

– Mom!

– Yes.

– Would you be so kind to nail my left hand to the table?

– Oh, my mom said.

***

I knew she wouldn't, and I wouldn't dare remain standing alone with my one hand nailed down and the other one free. I couldn't defend myself. In the end, all this would be too painful. It's true that hands are hands, but what hurts them also hurts me. I'm the victim of my own organism. My hands, lungs, kidneys—they're all plotting to do away with me, and I behave as if all this was no concern of mine and I'm even helping them destroy me with my writing. For days I haven't written a single line. If I had not started sinking, who knows when I would have mustered up the courage to write. Today or tomorrow my hands will cut my wrists or I'll hang myself or put a hundred pills in my mouth. And where did I lose so much time? I'm ashamed to admit it: in my vain attempts to light a cigarette. There were other reasons too, but this is the main one. I was getting ready to start writing and then I felt like smoking a cigarette. I put it into my mouth. The only thing that was left to do was strike the match, when the problem appeared: the matches were on my right, and I didn't have my right hand to grab them. Both my hands were there, but not my right one. I felt one and then the other. The right one was just not there. Of course, I started sinking, this is what the situation was like, and I'm positive that this sinking was more horrible than last night's sinking, because I didn't know with which hand I could hold on to some object, and even if I knew, it wouldn't help me at all, because the right hand wasn't showing up. I don't know when, how, or why it all ended. But, I finally figured out what happened: I was sitting and it seemed as though I was looking at my own reflection in the mirror. And all this, from the very beginning, was pretty stupid because I don't smoke. I have to admit: I'm still sitting on the edge of the bed (now it's only the bed) like an idiot with the dried-up cigarette in my mouth. And, needless to say, I'm writing. I have to write so that I won't die and I have to keep repeating this, repeating this, repeating this . . . so that I won't . . .

***

– Fritz!

– Yes, Mom.

– The two guys came here looking for you.

– What did they look like?

– Just ordinary.

– What did they want?

– They asked where you were.

– What did you say?

– I said I didn't know.

– What did they say?

– They'll come back soon.

***

"It's open," somebody says and I enter, as if in a dream, going straight towards the place from which the sounds of Mozart's sonata are coming. Moira is sitting at her piano, her back

turned towards me. Judging by her shoulders,

which are trembling spas

mod ically I conclude that she is crying. Then

with lots of sadness in her voice she says:

"The dream came true." "But dreams don't come true," I tried to explain to her.

"Dreams are like . . ."

Moira says:

"You came the following day and you were wearing a blue coat and black bow tie."

And indeed, I'm wearing a blue coat and a black bow tie, but that was yesterday.

I'm going to her, taking measured steps, and I kiss
 her neck.

Very gently. She turns around and from close up
I see that she reminds me of somebody.

I don't pay any attention to this. I'm carrying her to the couch and kissing her ear.

Suddenly

We're lying naked on the floor and all I can see is that

One Moira

Is lying next to me, the other Moira is crying and playing
 the piano, the third

Moira is saying, "It's open." The fourth

Moira is standing by the window and with the sharp
 razor
 is cutting
 her wrists . . .

***

Mom said they would come back soon. And I'm wasting my time. Do I really think somebody may be interested in unimportant details from my life? No. I have to write what they want. Well all right, I was born during the war because in war everything is allowed. My father? Unknown. Or a few of them. Or all of them together. My mom couldn't say no. She, also unknown, disappeared some place so that she could go on with her not being able to say *no*, until she died in an asylum for the mentally ill. I believe she pretended she was mentally ill so that she would be able to die in a bed, under a roof, in warmth. I don't blame her for anything. When times are tough, human beings have to do what they can in order to die. These were all misunderstandings. And this is how I look:

like a cubist picture, very abstract! I'm the hybrid of unknown fathers and misunderstandings. This is how I look from an angular point of view. Even if she couldn't say *no*, I assume she said *do not come inside*. Nobody paid any attention to what she said. That's because she did not mean it. And the sounds of bullets were whizzing by. And out of this lack of concentration, I was conceived. I spent nine months in the womb of that woman being poisoned by the alcohol from her blood, which, in a way, is my blood too. Without any doubt, this has been the hardest part of my life. An abortion could have solved everything. But it didn't. I repeat: misunderstanding after misunderstanding. It all tumbled down on my head. All this dirtiness. The fathers died or they were shot. My mom too. It's not their concern anymore. It was never their concern. And I have to live, I have to wear myself out decently to be able to die, to close my eyes, and finally blessed, surrender myself to the disintegration of my name, shape, sight and hearing. I have to die a couple of times so that all these things can disintegrate. I have to start loving my own death. I have to learn it by heart. I have to get an *A* in dying. Only then will this disappearance disappear. Nonetheless, it's awful to die. That's why I am where I am (if I am here); I'm here to keep on dying night after night until it becomes a routine. I'm here to study closely my own death and to write. But let's talk about it later. Now we're talking about my life. I was born a long time ago; you could say I'm thirty years old, but no you'd rather say I'm forty, fifty at most. There are no written documents, so it turns out that I live illegally. Perhaps that's why they ordered me to write. Later on it all got settled somehow. I got my first and last name. I can't remember where I was during the war. At that time I still didn't have a memory. In any case, I was neutral. Nobody can blame me for anything. I might have spent those years curled up in some cave, feeling numb, like a larva. Who knows? My memory starts in the orphanage. This is where it all begins. I was there until—but let's talk about this later. This is where I got used to the presence of other human beings. I lost this habit in time. One spermatozoid, you see, made its way through all the obstacles to the ovum and I used this opportunity, I rushed from my death to have some kind of existence. A really sad past. What's even sadder than this—I invented it.

★★★

– Mommmm!

– Yes?

– Where were you during the war?

– I was here.

– What were you doing?

– Nothing. What would I do?

– And where was I?

– You weren't born then.

– But where was I?

– !?

★★★

This is how I look from the outside: I'm hunched, skinny, and drooped over in a stiff coat that was out-of-fashion before it was even made. My most distinctive feature: glasses with thick lenses that don't need eyes at all—eyes are only an excuse for them; just as my coat doesn't need me, I am there, pro forma, because coats need people to be able to walk around. This is the way things are: coats and dresses—they all walk around, lie, love, and steal: and uniforms arrest and shoot. People just have minor roles in all this.

***

On my legs I have shoes that are made stronger by steel nails. Under my coat, I have my vest and trousers. I could write for hours about my trousers. What an impossible shape they have: they are wide around the waist, and at the ankles narrow, with huge cuffs. And the pattern—it's black material with dark red stripes. No doubt it's a pair of idiotic pants. In the whole city only I and the merchant—a Jew—in whose dark shop I worked at, and about whom I will say a few words now, because I remember the details—wear such pants. Before the Manager of the zoo took me with him, I worked with this loser, who reminded me of the Ukraine, because he had three golden teeth and kept smiling broadly and sadly until two, three or at most four years ago when he died of tuberculosis in a musty room behind his shop full of useless objects that nobody needed (just as nobody needed this Jew) but which we tried to sell in vain. As time goes by, I doubt more and more that this Jew ever existed. Because, what is left in my memory? Just the funny striped trousers and the wide smile with three golden teeth. If he did exist, I believe he won't make the same mistake again; I want to say: he'll never exist again, if you're still able to make choices after you die of tuberculosis. I believe in this because he didn't want anything, he didn't have any aspirations, while we weren't trying very hard to sell the useless objects from his shelves. We would sit the whole day in his shop, not because we were hoping we'd sell something, but because we were hoping that sooner or later another day would pass. And he would always laugh: in winter, in summer, in the morning, in the evening; he'd have a big smile and that reminded me of the Ukraine. Now, when I'm looking at my past from an angular point of view, I'm sure he was laughing at the stupid, hypocritical world in which people are simply forced to be Jews, Cherkezians, Hotentots or Germans, and in which they have to speak their own languages that make them unable to express anything. I never talked to my employer. We simply needed each other: I needed him for food and he needed me to help him not sell anything in his musty shop. We couldn't even talk. I didn't know Yiddish, and he didn't understand the language in which I spoke. I doubt he knew Yiddish. I would rather say he was thinking about some beautiful language of smiles. I'm sure he was laughing while he was dying. I'm not sure if he existed, but I'm sure he died with a smile on his face wide as the wide fields of the Ukraine. I'm crying here in my story, crying over his fate, crying over my eventual fate; I'm crying, wondering what kind of things a human being is forced to do; how many things they have to invent; how many sad events they have to recollect; how many wounds they have to reexperience to be able to write a lousy hundred pages of text.

***

And then one day the Manager of the zoo found himself in the musty store. I remember everything as if it happened yesterday. He was looking around the shop in his green coat. He was asking the price of this and that. He looked me in the eye, thought deeply, and asked: "Would you like to come with me?"

***

"Yes," I said.

***

The Manager took me to his home. From the window of his drawing room you could see the zoo. Every afternoon he played the piano. He wanted me to learn to play the piano. I didn't want to. I didn't like music. I spent my mornings alone. The Manager was feeding lions. I was looking from the window of the drawing room. The lions were unusually tame. The Manager liked the lions. He liked all the animals, but he liked the lions best. He wanted me to study painting. I didn't want to. I didn't like paintings. And then one afternoon the Manager stopped playing, he took me by the hand, and said: "These are the hands of a writer. Would you like to be a writer?" It sounded interesting. "Yes," I said. "I want to be a writer."

***

The Manager bought me a Remington typewriter.

***

I never wrote more than two, three or four sentences at most.

***

And it has been like this for ten years now.

***

And the Manager died. It happened one Thursday. Suddenly it wasn't November anymore. It was January. To make this more convincing, let's say it was snowing all day. I don't know, I really don't know how to write all this down. His death didn't come as a surprise to anybody; in the last few years he was bedridden, and we communicated using Morse code; he didn't move from his bed, his eyes were on the back of his head, and yet this still *was* the Manager, my benefactor, the only man who believed I'd become a writer one day. At first I didn't believe he died; I hit his head with my fists, I tickled his feet with a feather. Then I realized that he wasn't pretending. I didn't know how to behave in the presence of a dead man. I mean that I didn't know what the rituals were. I didn't know what to do. I was sitting despondently. For the first time in my life it became clear to me that it is very hard to be dead, cold, stiff. What I mean is it's hard for people who are left behind. There was no way for me to know what the Manager felt, if he felt anything. He suffered from unbearable headaches, which eventually killed him. I was hoping that death would bring an end to his headaches. In his head there was some terrible thing growing. A doctor told me this. I didn't take him seriously. I don't know, I really don't know how I'm going to write all these things down. I was left all alone in the world, not counting the dead body, left all alone. Thinking about all the things that he did for me, I wanted to lie down next to him, to have unbearable headaches, the terrible thing growing in my head, I wanted to die out of gratitude. I just couldn't figure it out: how is it possible that a man breathes—at least he's breathing—and then suddenly he doesn't breathe? I don't know, I really don't know how I'm going to describe all this; all these years when the Manager was bedridden, not able to say a word; all these years during which we communicated by Morse code tapping the signals with pencils, me on the table, he on his headboard. It lasted five, perhaps ten or at most fifteen years. It took time until the tumor in the Manager's head grew so large that it killed him. And finally, that Thursday the Manager died; he closed his eyes and left his corpse, about which I didn't know what to do. The Manager was already dead for too long, and I should have done something about his funeral before the warm days set in; I was hoping that by that time I'd be able to find a reasonable explanation for the Manager's great wish to be buried face-down; that's what he wrote in his will: I wouldn't know how to invent all this.

It was time I started thinking.

***

I started thinking and a completely new, magical world opened up before me.

***

Every night I would lock myself in my room and read Agatha Christie novels.

V

"There's a letter for you," my brother-in-law is yelling from the kitchen.

Letter—of course. Blue, registered, official and it says:

Fritz, or Fin or Fi, or whatever your name may be.

It's no use changing names. We know all your names. We know everything about you. We aren't interested in you. We just want your hundred or so double-spaced pages. We do not care at all what you write about. At a certain time we have to submit the manuscript. That's all. Time is slipping by, and you are making little progress.

Please take note:

It's none of our business but we think that you would make more progress if you stop hanging out with the girls from your neighborhood.

At your age. Shame on you!

Illegible signatures

Post scriptum

We'll come back soon.

***

How on earth did they find out that my name is not Fritz anymore?

– Idiots, persecutors, killers, goons!

I am yelling at the top of my lungs. And again:

– Idiots, persecutors, killers, goons!

***

The walls of my room have strained their ears and they are trying to hear what I'm saying.

***

There was nothing else I could do. I called myself Fritz again.

***

By the window, a wide red pool of blood is spreading around, and it seems to me that I will ride over the roofs on Moira . . .

Just shadows . . .

Two days after

The postman brings a letter for me again. By the light pink envelope I recognize who it is from. There is no need to look at the slightly slanted handwriting:

I do not know if you have heard that I cut my wrists. I feel ashamed. I feel better now and soon I will be discharged, but I do not feel like leaving. I would rather stay here because unsuccessful suicide attempts are not looked at approvingly. I am afraid that my tendons have been hurt so much that I won't be able to play the piano anymore. And if I do, it won't be like it used to be. I would like you to visit me.

M.

***

After six days I hear the sounds of the piano again. So, she came out. She is playing "Fascination." But she isn't playing very well and stops quickly. A heavy silence envelops the whole building. I assume that behind the walls Moira is crying.

***

All night long you can hear in Moira's room a wild stomping. But it's not a herd of horses. It's the galloping tuberculosis.

***

"Dear listeners, it's six o'clock. News."

***

My God, she's still leaving. I realized this last night. I came home, took off my legs, then my skin, sat on the edge of the bed and covered my face with my hands. How could I have been so stupid to think that all this will end one day, that several years will be enough for her to leave, and for me to forget everything. Now I can be sure: she's leaving, she's leaving and nothing can stop her, she's leaving this text just as she's done before. She was always leaving. She came with the intention to leave. She'd change names, change features, change her voice, she'd come back disguised; when I forgot she was leaving, she'd leave me sitting on the edge of my bed/madness with my hands on my face. To remind me that she'd be leaving forever. Only yesterday I realized everything: All of them were she, one and only. I hate these hands on my face, this crumpled face under my hands. I hate all her faces, all her hands in my cowardly hands that know nothing else but to hold her hands and cover up my face.

***

They don't even know how to kill me.

I should write down my plan for tomorrow. So that I don't forget.

***

7:00	get up
8:00	breakfast
9:00	return books to the library
9:00-14:00	write the text
14:00-16:00	go for a walk
16:00-17:00	write letters
17:30	tear up the letters
17:30-19:30	walk up and down the room
19:30-21:30	sit on the edge of the bed
21:30-22:00	make necessary preparations
22:00	muster up the courage
22:15	hang myself

***

Mom, I didn't hang myself. It doesn't surprise me at all. Lately I haven't been able to do even a third of all the things that I planned. Is it because I masturbate a lot? I even plan things that exceed my ability to do. For example, I got up around 8:30 and already my schedule was disrupted. I had my breakfast at 9:00. After that I vomited. I was greedy. I ate four sheets of paper together with my breakfast. At 10:15, I went to the library to return books, but there was nobody there because it was Sunday. Even if it was a business day, I doubt I'd have the courage to go in and return books because I had kept them for the past ten years, and I just didn't have the courage to return them after all this time. Agatha Christie novels. I didn't even write the letters, Mom. I didn't write the letters until 13:00, and then it was too late to start writing. The pencils were very dull, and my Remington typewriter does not type on Sundays. I was even late for my walk. Still, it's not all hopeless. I walked up and down my room and I was sitting on the edge of my bed. I covered my face with my hands. I managed to do *something* at least. It wasn't until evening that I went out into the street (later I will say what happened). When I came back home I was tired. I sat on the edge of the bed, I tried to muster up the courage but it didn't work. I didn't hang myself. It doesn't mean that the night went by in vain. I spent this time sitting on the edge of the bed fearing death, which, to some degree, is the same thing as hanging myself, if not worse. I'm sure it is worse. Death lasts for a short time. And fear—it lasts and lasts, Mom. I wanted to hang myself, thinking that my situation has become unbearable. Now I know that it's never unbearable. It's unbearable only to a certain extent. And then it stops. But this limit isn't exactly defined. It is elastic. It yields before the avalanches of unbearable things until it wipes itself out. Each time it's more unbearable, each time it's unbearable in a different way. You shouldn't pay attention to this. Mom, I was reading the Bible. I guess I wanted to console myself. After I realized what it is that I need to redeem myself, I thought that it would be better if I killed myself, if I died instantly, rather than spending the rest of my life fearing punishment. Why didn't I kill myself? Why does nothing work for me? Mom, what am I to do, Mom?

***

– Fritz!

– Yes, Mom?

– Come here.

– Why?

– Two guys are here looking for you.

***

– We're here.

– I see.

– And?

– I still haven't finished.

– We thought so.

– Why did you come then?

– Because you were supposed to give us your manuscript today.

– And what now? I haven't finished yet.

– What page did you get to?

– 53.

The bigger one (the one who always does the talking) looks at his friend. "What shall we do?" he asks. He shrugs his shoulders, takes out a kind of notebook, goes through it, looks furtively at me and says: "Let's give him some more time."

– All right. You've got some more time.

On his way out, he stops at the door and says: "We'll come back soon."

***

– Fritz!

– Yes, Mom.

– Who were those two guys?

– They came for the statement.

– Fritz!

– Yes, Mom.

– What have you done, what have you done, what have you done, what have you done, what have you done . . .

– Nothing, Mom, nothing.

***

This thing yesterday . . . It was a fascination. Now I know. First, I was mad at everybody. "I hate you!" I was yelling inside while being squeezed by the crowds in the street. "I hate what you look like, your suits, the excrement inside you, your harlequin caps. I hate your fear of death that will erase you from the face of this world; I feel ashamed of myself when I'm afraid of death." I was feeling ashamed, of course, because I wasn't doing anything except being afraid of death. I was repulsed by this fear, I was tired of this endless anxiety. "All right," I thought. "Whatever happens, happens." I decided to die and I was no longer afraid of death. I went into the cathedral to take a rest. I was sitting in the pleasant shade of the half-empty church watching the hunched sexton's daughter put out almost-burnt candles with some very useful device. This kind of insultingly transparent face you can meet only in empty cathedrals. She was a friend from school. How else could I know that she was the sexton's daughter? After putting out the candles, she disappeared down some aisle. I followed her. She was waiting for me in a recess in the wall. "You know," I said, "we have been studying for years together and it is only today that I discovered that you are beautiful." She didn't say anything. She was crying. The tears were rolling down her gypsum face. With surprise I realized that I wasn't lying: she really was beautiful. Until then, I was lying. She wasn't a friend from school. But I didn't lie when I said she was beautiful. As always happens when I'm not lying, I couldn't say a word. I was speechless. If I don't want to lie, I have to keep quiet. It's not possible the other way around. She was crying, I was silent. God is my witness. He, crucified over the altar, was silent too. I don't know how long it took before she ran away. The Mass had started. The organist was playing "Shine on You Crazy Diamond." While I was going between rows of pews, the priest looked at me with hatred because the candles went out, the wax spilled over and the whole inside of the church looked as if it were sprinkled with sperm.

***

This was a fascination. Now I know. I went out, it was already night, a whole night in which I wouldn't have to be afraid of death. But let me not exaggerate: I was still sad. I went to a bar to have a beer, feeling sad that I wouldn't be able to write even a hundredth, a thousandth part of all the pleasant things that were happening to me. This is how things are: I can express myself only about matters like fear of death or melancholy. And then She appeared. She walked into the bar, sat down at the table near the entrance, and ordered tea. I can't say anything about her looks. Or I can: as if an angel from the cathedral came down from its pedestal to have tea in a semi-dark bar.

***

"Allow me please to sit down," I said kindly. "My name is Salajdin Bejs."

***

I revealed my true name. Her dress, made of sparkling beads, was blinding me and I couldn't clearly see her face. The bar owner brought two pink candles. "What, what's your name?" she asked me, her ear getting closer and closer to my mouth. "My name is Salajdin, Salajdin Bejs."

***

"Strange name."

***

Really, a strange name: Salajdin Bejs.

***

"Well, Salajdin, tell me about yourself," she said with a smile on her face—one of those smiles that seem so cliché in a story. But then . . . then this smile made me talk, talk, talk . . .

***

"You won't believe it. Yesterday I wanted to hang myself, and tonight I'm happy. Tomorrow I'll want to hang myself again. But I won't hang myself. I'm not even able to do that. I'm so apathetic. Depressed. Nothing works for me. You see, I have to finish a manuscript, some kind of a statement, I need a hundred double-spaced pages, and I've just made it past the fiftieth page. I don't know where I found the courage to say what I'm going to say right now: If you were by my side, if I could see you for only a couple of minutes every week, everything would be completely different. I'm sure that it's only you who can pull me out of my nightmares, my melancholy; only you can save me from my doubts that are slowly driving me crazy. But I know all this is just castles in the air. Vain dreams, as Joyce would say at the end of *Finnegans Wake*. And you see, even now, now when I don't believe that my sitting next to you is real, I play stupid word games. I know that this is a castle in the air because you are beautiful, and I'm so ugly, stupid and apathetic . . .

***

– Listen to what I'm going to tell you, Salajdin. (Her lips were quite close to my ear.) Even you yourself don't believe what you're saying. As far as I can see, you're lost among your sentences, your head is spinning from the leaps they are making, you even thought that this world you're talking about is real. You even invented the two guys who are forcing you to write whatever you're writing. You're not capable of doing anything because what you want is only in your imagination. And your nightmares are only in your imagination. And your anxieties are only in your imagination. You've been trying to separate dream from reality in vain, because in sentences there is neither reality nor dreams.

– Well, then you're in my imagination too.

– I'm not.

– How can I trust you?

– I don't know. You have to believe, if you want to meet me again.

– And when can I see you again?

– When you finish writing your hundred pages of text and submit your manuscript.

– And you? What's your name?

– You'll find out when you meet me again.

– So, when my story is ready, you'll come back?

– I'll be back.

– How can I be sure?

– Remember! The murderer always returns to the scene of the crime.

★★★

"We're closing," the bar owner said.

★★★

"And when did the girl who was sitting with me leave?"

★★★

"Did you hear me, you son of a bitch, we're closing! Don't make me say this again."

★★★

This was a fascination. Now I know.

***

In my apartment I found the past perfect tense: my sister and her mongoloid husband had been sleeping enveloped in a heavy, sweaty smell, and then it all suddenly turned into simple past tense: with all my strength I kicked their bed and they woke up. The mongoloid mumbled something unintelligible, though sufficiently intelligible for me to understand that he hates me. I hate him too. And my sister. This was the only way it could be before I finished my manuscript. I hated the mongoloid just because his father was a butcher. There was nothing wrong with his father. He even wrote songs. I needed a reason to hate him. Nothing else. I knew that tomorrow I'd feel ashamed because I woke them up, but tomorrow was still far away. I locked myself in my room and started fearing death again. Down there, in his butcher shop, the mongoloid's father has already butchered all the sheep for tomorrow. All he had to do was cut them in half, hang them on the spikes, then go home, lock himself in his room, and write long, sad songs until dawn about the girl looking through the window, all misty with rain, at the street.

***

Next scene: Morning, my room, my mom and me.

Mom: Fritz, what was it that you were writing yesterday? I haven't read anything so stupid as that in a long time. You have no style, your sentences are undeveloped, and your plan to deconstruct a literary text hasn't been achieved. These couple of pages are the weakest parts in your story.

I: But Mom, all this really happened.

Mom: Don't talk nonsense. How could anything have happened when you were writing the whole night?

I: But tell me, since when did you become a literary critic?

Mom: A couple of years ago.

I: Have you published anything?

Mom: No.

I: So, you're not competent enough.

Mom: I can prove to you that in the subtext . . .

I: Mom, stop the bullshit.

Director (aside): But noooo, but nooo! Too pathetic. Too dilettante. Fritz, you have to become serious, and anyway you shouldn't use that language with your mom.

I (to myself): Shit! My name is Fritz again.

Director: Here we go again!

The same scene: Morning, my room, my mom and me.

Mom: Fritz, where were you yesterday?

I: I was with a beautiful girl.

Mom: What's the name of this beauty?

I: I don't know. I call her Luna.

Mom: Do you believe in what you're saying?

At this moment I jump up screaming. I climb the armoire and hide behind the jars of jam, all the time screaming so that I wouldn't be able to say: *I don't believe.*

Director: That's much better.

***

"Dear listeners, you have been listening to a radio play . . ."

***

I turn off the radio.

***

It was a fascination. Now I know.

VI

Again I just wasted three or four days. I can hardly remember how. I only remember going out for a walk after having spent the whole night in a state of panic thinking about death. I sat on a park bench and then I thought I had an idea that I should write down. I took out the notebook, put it on my knees and wrote: I sat on a park bench and then I thought I had an idea that I should write down. I took out the notebook, put it on my knees and wrote . . . But, the idea seemed to have completely disappeared! While I was writing that I had an idea, I forgot what I really wanted to write, I want to say—I forgot what this idea was about, so I spent the whole day and night writing about how I sat on a park bench and how I thought I had an idea that I should write down. I just couldn't get rid of the awful endless repetitive pattern because the sentence went in a circle and always ended with an inevitable colon, which, as we know, is not the way a sentence should end. The very idea that started all this soon lost its importance. The only important thing was to get out of this hopeless sentence, and I couldn't simply finish it, because in that case there'd be something left unsaid, and I wouldn't know what I really wanted to say. My notebook filled up quickly, and so I used the bench. I wrote all over it. With the unsharpened half of my pencil I continued writing on the hard ground. My memory doesn't reach back any further than this. I must have somehow found a way to finish the sentence (I couldn't have started the next one otherwise), but I repeat: I don't remember how I finished the sentence. It might have been a tragic end. Anyway, I found myself in front of the door of my room this morning. I wish I would have found at least myself *in* the room. I needed some company, even lousy company. Of course, I wasn't there. I'm always in the wrong place. I only found a rat squatting on the table and nibbling at the pages. This outraged me enormously. I decided to kill it, to take its skin off, to dismember it, burn it, pour acid over it, but my rage made me clumsy (the only time my hands aren't clumsy is when I'm the one who needs to be killed), so I had enough time to calm down and think about everything. In the end, what is it that I have against this rat? Isn't this rat just an unhappy man after all? And what better purpose was there for the pages of my statement than to feed the rat? I gave the rat some clean paper. It trembled with fear. "Don't be afraid," I said as gently as I could. "I won't harm you." But he didn't have a name. I should have come up with a name for him. I called him Fritz because such a generic name provokes sympathy. Then I went out. I went out of the room again so that I wouldn't kill myself instead of Fritz—the rat. As a precaution I didn't take my notebook with me. I went to the river, stood on the bridge and looked at the muddy water of something that was supposed to be a river and tried to bring into harmony what I felt and what I saw. You see, I started writing one, two, perhaps three months ago; *today* I don't exist anymore nor did I exist *yesterday*, let alone a month, two, or three ago. This is what is utterly devaluing the writing: discontinuity among thoughts, events and what was written about them. On paper everything has its direction, its logic, but in reality everything that happens except for this logic is unclear. I have nothing in common with the destiny of my life. I have nothing in common with what I am writing right now. It's an awful thing to say, but it has to be said: Things that have never happened before are always happening—and as soon as they happen—they disappear and never happen again. Still, something else happens. Always something else happens. For example:

F
A
L
L
S

Something is happening, something quite irrelevant, but based on the same principle, the most important things in our lives are happening. And again something happens. Can it be different? It's not that I don't know what—this happening, but still there is nothing else left for me to do. My day, after all, was not so bad. I'm not dead. My heart is beating, my lungs are inhaling and exhaling, my blood is circulating, my kidneys are purifying my blood, the Earth is revolving. This almost makes me feel dizzy. How's all this possible? All this can't go on by itself—the revolving of the Earth, the beating of the heart, and the inhaling and exhaling of the lungs. I better not think about this. If you think really carefully about something, it immediately becomes clear to you that it is nothing.

***

"Don't try to feel your pulse or you'll ruin something," the rat from the wastepaper basket tells me.

***

And during that time *that quite irrelevant thing* that was happening—happened. It FELL. Boom! It was a flowerpot. I guess it didn't hit anyone. I correct myself: nothing irrelevant ever happens. One event sets into motion another event. No matter how irrelevant an event may seem at first glance, it causes an unpredictable series of other events. Unfortunately, the flowerpot hit a man on the head. Let's say that this man is some guy, call him *X*. X fell on the ground covered in blood. A passerby saw this, and his conscience made him call an ambulance (though he was in a hurry); he lost time doing that, and he was late for the meeting with his fiancée. The fiancée got angry, she decided to leave the passerby, and got married to somebody else. But, the destiny of an accidental passerby is not our business. What happened to X? X hemorrhaged. The ambulance was rushing towards the place of the accident. Since the ambulance has priority, lots of other cars had to let the ambulance pass, but a thirty-second delay caused disturbances in an already existing course of the events. So what happened was that a car ran into the passerby and it wouldn't have run into him if it wasn't for this delay. Another car ran into a parked truck and the driver was instantly killed. But this isn't all. It's not the millionth part of what the fall of an ordinary flowerpot caused. Since the ambulance didn't get there in time, X died of a cerebral hemorrhage. Of course, he had to be buried. This is how things are usually done. They buried him in the only remaining lot in the city cemetery. Whoever died next didn't have a place to be buried in. His family had to use connections. They paid the administrator in charge to dig up some old grave. Somebody noticed this and the result was quite an unpleasant affair. Not to mention that the doctor who couldn't save X started drinking, and he was drinking so much that his wife left him and asked for a divorce. His kids became neurotic. One of them became a sullen sadist who brings lots of suffering on his family, and the other one a manic-depressive who could take a gun at any minute and shoot into a crowd. It's better not to think about these things. It's better to assume that the pot never fell and go back to the bridge. So, I was standing on the bridge and suddenly a thought flashed through my mind—I shouldn't be on this Earth at all. If the Earth is where I belong, I guess it would have felt good to be here. But I just feel anxious on this Earth.

***

My mom bursts into my room. "You are just sitting and writing, wasting your time doing stupid things, and your sister is getting a divorce!"

***

Getting a divorce? So soon? She got along so well with the mongoloid. They were an excellent couple. Every night they took a stroll by the river. They always held hands. Now they are getting divorced. It's their business. I won't interfere.

***

"You whore, bitch, scum! You put shame on our house. What would your dead father say about all of this ? What will our neighbors say? What will the family say?"

***

Dead father?!

***

Mom, when did our father die?

***

My mother is crying . . .

***

Mom, why are you crying?

***

My mom is laughing.

***

July 23

Lord in Heaven,

I take the liberty to turn to You with a letter. My soul might burn in Eternal Hell because of this impertinence, but our existence in this world in this body is an excellent preparation for the tortures of Hell. Personally, I have no doubt that You created us human beings. Something so vain and conceited, something so stupid, could not just have been produced by a blind elemental force. No! Lots of thought has been put into a human being. But why? Why did You need us? You had your angels who could not sin. Why did You need a human being made of clay? In the end, if You needed the human species for some reason (which of course is unclear to me), why did You need me*? Couldn't everything have gone smoothly without* me*?*

But since I'm here, I would like You to explain to me, although this is not possible (I cannot picture a God who could talk to me), I would like You to explain to me how to put an end to this void around me.

You see, I met a girl the other night. You already know that because You are all-knowing. It seemed to me that she could bring me salvation. And what happened? She left, I don't know her name, nor her address and more and more I doubt that this has actually happened. Lord in Heaven, are your angels playing with me? Are they laughing at me?

Lord in Heaven,

I have only one prayer. Please let me finish these hundred pages and find this girl again.

The worst part of all is that, everything considered, we cannot die. Pushed from the void into existence, we can't go back to the void, and You are not letting us into reality.

What should I do?

Hoping for a favorable solution to my request,

Humbly yours,

S. B.

***

"There's a letter for you!" my mom yells. Letter—of course. Blue, registered, official, and in the letter it says:

Don't forget to solve the math problem.

We'll come back soon!

Illegible seal

Illegible signature

***

2x2=4, 4x4=16, 47-24=23, 36÷2=18

Practiced the whole morning. Thank God, I am through with half of it already.

***

"Fritz," my typewriter says to me. "Don't you think we should get some rest?"

VII

The bus was unbearably crowded. It suited me very well. I bypassed the ticket collector in order to avoid paying. I admit it. I didn't have any money. Holding onto the handrail, I felt somebody's breasts on my elbow. I turned around and saw an ugly face, almost as ugly as mine, ugly—if not also pathetic—like the mongoloid face of my anxiety. The bus was just going by the big, multicolored F, then U, then N, then P, then A, then R, then K. The letters of the sign made of multicolored bulbs lit up in this order, and the bus was passing them by. For the moment I saw smiling faces, and then they *disappeared* behind the huge gray building. I pushed my way forward. The owner of the ugly face followed me and again I felt her breast on my elbow. I can't write anything about how I felt about this. Still, let me try. I might have experienced a temporary split in my personality. As if there were two separate *I*'s inside my ordinary, worn-out *I*. The one exalted, the other one humiliated because of the first one who subconsciously tried to find the way to take the owner of the ugly face out of the bus and kiss her in a dark cellar, to touch her *labia maiora* in order to prove that he knows Latin and to say all those nonsensical things that usually accompany groping in the dark. All this lasted for just a moment. It lasted far less than these sentences about it. The bus was passing the city cemetery. The spirits of my friends, relatives, and acquaintances were hovering around. I got off at the next stop. I fed Fritz. Fritz-me, or Fritz-the rat? I don't know. I wanted to hang myself again. But I couldn't. The human being who isn't able to commit suicide—doesn't deserve to live. But here is the question: Would I have hanged the right man if I had really hanged myself? What am I? It's impossible to say anything about me. Whatever I say, it's not me anymore. In the past I used to think, I used to convince myself that *I* is not I; I have to admit that I got rid (although for just a little bit) of the unbearable burden of the reflexive pronoun *myself*, but the pronoun (as its name suggests) always returned to me each time, even more perfidious, more malicious than before. I couldn't get used to *I*. What *I* want I does not want. It feels disgusted. As if I had somebody in my body working to destroy it. To make it go insane. This *I* is a parasite. It feels comfortable. My *I* is on the edge of a nervous breakdown. It happens that I find myself standing on the corner of the street for hours without being able to move, to go where some urgent business is taking me just because this *I* wants to go somewhere else. I would have killed myself if I only knew that this other *I* won't outlive me. But, how can I be sure about this? Isn't my handwriting getting smaller and smaller? Am I not already writing in such small letters that my handwriting, if I continue in this way, will turn into a simple illegible line on paper—which will best express my feelings?

***

I come home. My sister is sitting and crying. "What happened?" I ask. She's still crying. She isn't able to say a word. I slap her face and she says: "White slave merchants kidnapped our mom!"

***

As if I didn't have enough of my own problems. But this could be my mother after all.

In a cartoon, Hewey, Dewey, and Louie would be saying, "This is incredible! A 90-year-old woman kidnapped in broad daylight."

***

I'll have to do something about this as soon as possible. But what? Lately, an Arab has been seen on our street. Is he a clue to this mystery? Or was he sent to cover the tracks? He could be the clue. Arabs like blonde women. My mom is not blonde. But they could dye her hair.

***

I went to visit my friend in the Department of Pathology. “I haven’t seen you in a long time,” he said smiling. “You see”—he showed me the corpses on the tables—“all of them were alive when you last came here.” Yes. It was a long time ago. “I’m in trouble,” I confided in him. “What’s the matter?” “My mom has been kidnapped by white slave merchants.” “Pretty awful,” the pathologist said after a short silence. “Really awful stuff.” “And what’s your advice?” My friend was thinking while he was dissecting somebody’s brain. Then he said: “The best thing for you would be to go to the white slave market in Susangerd and buy your mother.”

***

It’s nice to have friends.

***

– But I don’t have money.

– You won’t need much money for that. Don’t get me wrong, but your mom is an elderly woman, and they’re not really that expensive. I’m sure that with a little money you can have your mom again.

– But I don’t have enough money to go to the white slave market in Susangerd.

– Look, Salajdin, what a wonderful brain specimen.

– I said I don't have enough money to go to Iran.

– Oh. You can hitchhike.

***

I didn't have time for coffee. I had to do something as soon as possible. Still, I had enough time to think about how many of them (the ones who were healthy and alive right now) will lie under my friend's scalpel next time I come to visit him.

***

I got up the courage but instead of going to Susangerd I went to the police station.

– Good afternoon, I say.

– Good afternoon, the cop on duty says. What do you need?

– I've come to report a kidnapping.

– Who's been kidnapped?

– My mom.

– Her name? the cop asks and takes out some official forms.

Problems. I can't remember my mom's name. I never called her by her name. Always and only: Mom. But how do I say this to the cop? How would he take it? Would he think I'm making a fool of myself? After all, cops don't like people who forget their mom's names.

– Her name is Izolda, I lie.

– Last name?

Is my mom's last name the same as mine? I have a couple of last names, but I will give just one. My guess might be right, and if I don't . . .

– Bejs.

– So, Izolda Bejs. Date of birth?

– I don't know. She is ninety years old.

– Her occupation?

– Literary critic.

– Is she pretty?

– Hmm. Not really.

– In that case the chances aren't good that we're going to find her. Ugly women are inconspicuous, nobody pays any attention to them, not even the police. Still, we'll do everything we can.

– I'm sorry, but have you read any absurdist plays by Eugene Ionesco?

– No. Who's that? Why do you ask?

– Because our conversation reminds me very much of the dialogs in his plays.

(Of course, the last two questions weren't asked.)

***

I'm going back home thinking about what to do when an Arab man appears in front of me. He is gesticulating to me that he needs matches.

– Do you know anything about white slave merchants? I ask.

- . . . . . , said the Arab man.

I didn't give him the matches. Perhaps he was involved in my mom's kidnapping.

***

And suddenly, as in a novel, I thought I saw Luna in a crowd of people. I run after her and, as in a novel, I don't catch up with her. She is lost somewhere, she disappears . . .

***

My God, I'm fooling around in this bizarre episode about the disappearance of my mom, and suddenly everything disappears.

***

I come home. My sister is sitting and howling with laughter. "What happened?" I ask. She is still howling with laughter. She can't say a word. I slap her face and she says: "White slave merchants returned our mom. They had the wrong address."

***

This is how the case ended. "The Kidnapping of Fritz's Mom."

In a cartoon Mickey would be saying to Goofy: "As of late the newspapers are full of lies!"

VIII

I'm stuck. I knew this would happen. I have to do all kinds of things in order to write. I spend the whole day in the street waiting for things to happen to me so that I'll have something to write about. Today, for example, I had a hard time until I noticed a girl without an arm. This isn't a particularly interesting theme, but I'm easy to please. At first glance there's nothing strange about this. All right! It's not unusual to see a creature without an arm or leg. It's not so terrible. What's terrible is that the people around them pretend not to notice this defect. They call this nice behavior. Pretending that you aren't noticing something as conspicuous as a missing arm is supposed to be an indicator of your good manners. But I don't think so. This is just the beginning of the process that results in some X or Y person passing unnoticed, overlooked, ignored. This is what I'm most afraid of: the end of persecution. And what happens to people who have some bodily defect? Instead of making their situation easier, we give them a job that even a person with no defect would find hard to do, and all this with the excuse that a disabled person won't feel useless this way. And what is this girl going to do in the world in which even two hands aren't enough to cover your face with? What if she wants to hide? To cry? Not to mention the small amount of attention we pay to those who don't exist. Losing a part of your body is a difficult thing, but even the loss of the whole body doesn't mean that you lose your personality. It's not possible to lose *I*. Death only makes trying to find your way around harder. Nobody takes the dead into account. Death brings lots of loneliness. I want to say: death has nothing to do with your personality. Life is something that *I* either have or don't have. Those who have it are people, those who don't have it are the ones who don't exist. Temporarily, of course. I talked about them already. You can (and should) exist quite nicely even without life. My friend X—whose full name I don't mention here out of respect for his family (though I doubt that they will ever read these lines)—committed suicide two years ago. He swallowed 30,000 barbiturates. After having been in a coma for three days his *body* expired in the Department of Neuropsychiatry. His consciousness, his *I*, passed out immediately after his body had been numbed with barbiturates. He swallowed them in a conscious effort to kill this body in which he couldn't stay anymore. And this body was kept alive (?) for seventy-two hours more. I'd like to know if the gentlemen psychiatrists, since they consider those who try to commit suicide to be mentally deranged, would think of the people who successfully commit suicide to be deranged as well. Do they think that their corpses are mentally deranged corpses? This is insane! But, what can you do? To die of your own will is considered to be the height of indecency according to proper etiquette. X, as I said, has left, nobody pays any attention to him now, they just *remember* him; it is as though somebody talked to a *version* of me a year ago, not to *me*. Such a man never existed. I'm always just a moment. And I'm fooling myself that I'm thirty, thirty-five, forty at most. I have nothing. Just my poor *I* constantly being bullied by its senses. In my head there is an incessant ticking, whistling: pi-piii, pi-piii, pi-piiii. Nothing serious. Just the Morse code. The telegram repeating for days: THERE IS SOMETHING WHISTLING IN YOUR HEAD STOP NOTHING SERIOUS STOP JUST THE USUAL TELEGRAM REPEATING FOR DAYS . . . STOP STOP. Luckily, there is a STOP! But my face won't be anything less than a crumpled bag because of that. It will go mad. Because I drink too much coffee. But what kind of coffee? This coffee is conspiring against me. I have a box of coffee on which it says FRANCK KAFA. Quite an ordinary box. But this is a perfidious anagram: FRANCK KAFA. It means—"The Trial." Why quotes? It's enough to say *the trial*. I hope it's clear to me what I wanted to say.

***

"The phone is for you!" my sister is yelling.

***

"Hello."

"Do you know who this is?"

(Of course I know. I could never forget this voice. This deep, velvety, female voice.)

"Of course I know. Where are you calling from?"

"From home. I wanted to ask you how you're getting along."

"Well, I made it to page 83."

"Oooo, this is better."

"Will I see you once I'm done with it?"

"Of course. I keep my promises. I wanted to tell you something else. You see, I . . . "

Click!

Pi-pii, pi-pii, pi-piii

"Hello, hello, hello . . ."

***

Fritz goes to his room and starts writing in his diary: "Fritz is standing by the telephone and he's crying."

***

Mad at everything. I'd like to read something, but it's making me sick. Yes, I read sometimes, I read because reading is a ritual like sleeping, eating, going to the theater, using the restroom: saying "Good afternoon, how are you," because more or less this is all part of a well-rehearsed life. But books, if I may say so, are just shit. Their only purpose is to allow the writers to live through the hell of this life and not feel it in their skin. The best books are either burnt or unpublished until the moment when they eventually get published—only to be burnt. There is a constant decline in real books. I mean the ones in which you can find real excitement or dangers. For example, the books that have machines from hell built into them, and if you really want to read them you have to detonate the mine. Or war books with hidden caplets of poisonous gas in them that require careful leafing through with a gas mask always at hand. Not so long ago, books quite seriously talked about abstractions like *honor*, *glory*, *love* (uh!), *courage*. What is happening nowadays is that books, in most cases, talk about dishonor, cowardice, and hatred, because it seems that readers have finally got it clear in their heads that they can never possibly be linked with positive things. And that's good. This is a progress. As far as I'm concerned, what I like reading most are books in Finnish or Norwegian, because I don't know these languages and because they provide me with so many new sounds. I read aloud and I listen to the sound of it. Everything is sound. Fine sound that we see, the sound which we hear, thick sticky sound that we can feel like the hardness of an object. Now let me be a philosopher for a while. I think that's all right. They said: *write!* They didn't say about what. Well, if I say "stone," this is just a word, this isn't something hard at all, but if thousands of generations in thousands, thousands of years keep endlessly repeating "stone," "stone," "stone," then the result of this is quite tangible rocks that you can crack windows with or somebody's head. None of these things are clear to me. And they shouldn't be clear to me. I start talking about books, and the sentences change the topic and start talking about sound and then about rocks. I want to say: Life is something so untested that it is mere idiocy to expect books, coming out of this life, to be anything else but a deception and a lie. In a world such as ours you can construct sentences with more or less logic to them, I admit this—but the question is how much logic there is in this world. Little. Unfortunately just a little. This much, this little, even less than this . . . much, much less than this . . .

***

And the dream? What's with the dream?

It feels like it was a long time ago or somewhere very far away when I was last awake. It was last night. I fell asleep early, exhausted because I was feeling scattered, listless, diffuse, unable to confront the abyss of nothingness that squeezed that negligible little *something* of myself threatening to pop it like a soap bubble. Dreaming now seems more real than being awake, which precedes it. Perhaps because an awful lot of time passed by. I grew old in my dream. My dead friends died again, those who are still alive went around with pale smiles on their faces. Moira cut her veins again. I was sitting with Luna (let's say

Luna) again in a stuffy bar and all of them were peering through the windows, knocking with their fingers on the windowpanes and, like deaf mutes, moving their lips, they said: "I am dead, I am dead." And then all of them (both males and females) left one by one, and disappeared. Just like in the real world. I caught up with them in a corridor that had no end in sight. But I couldn't catch up with them. Nobody could catch up with anybody. We all walked forward without any possibility of turning back and seeing who was behind us. For a long, long time. On both sides of the corridor there was a long line of doors. I knocked on each of them, opened them, checked *if I was there*, kept going, and it went on like this for years, my being tired of countless births, worn out by countless deaths, with no hope that I'll ever find what I'm looking for . . .

There, that is what it is like in my dream.

***

– Why don't you read something to me? my sister says.

– What did you say? You haven't shown interest in literature before.

– I can't fall asleep. So, this might help.

– Well, OK. I will read to you:

"This world, the way it is, is the way it is just out of pure habit. They taught us in school: the Danube flows into the Black Sea; Bucharest is the capital of Romania; Mont Blanc is such and such tall. Let anyone dare claim something different. They will end up in an asylum of course. Nobody checks whether all this is true. But what happens sometimes is that this world sinks; suddenly it starts crumbling and falling down on me. This is what I'd like to read to you, my dear sister with a failed marriage behind you: About our infinite loneliness in this world. Death is just a disintegration of one person's perspective on the world. This is what I'll present to the Academy of Sciences one day. I will say: if there is no perspective on the world, there is no death. Unfortunately, it's very hard, almost impossible, not to have a perspective on this world. Even going crazy is just another perspective, somewhat more sincere however, behind the bars of a madhouse. It's possible to crumple your face, throw it on the floor, step on and spit on it but that doesn't solve anything. There'll be nothing left of you in the eyes of other masks, but *this* death will still be at work on you. The only solution is to get smaller. If I keep on getting smaller, I'll lose all size. When I lose my size, I'll become a zero; when I become a zero, I'll become everything. What will be left of me is just the rest of it. In this case, death doesn't find anything. It goes away feeling ashamed. It's not working anymore. My arrogant coat feels heavier and heavier. But it plays a very important role. That's why I put up with it. The way it is always tight on me, buttoning it all the way up makes me unable to relax. Comfort spoils people. It's very important to have some kind of burden. Some kind of obstacle, something that constantly reminds you that there is a body that needs to be taken care of. If I take my coat off, I'd immediately start thinking in a diffuse way and soon fall asleep. The uneasiness makes me feel *it*, bear with it, so that my thoughts can freely think about everything. My thoughts most frequently think about disappearing; they think I don't think enough about death, that my avoiding the subject of death is not a reflection of courage or carelessness, but of the mere cowardice, and of fear of coming face to face with it. Think of all the things that we do in the hospitals so that people can heal and die healthy. And death is just some general place. That's how they treat it. Since everybody shuns it, what is left is only life, the order inside life, birth registries, records, card catalogs beyond which life doesn't even exist. Everything is being recorded. Even the smallest detail of somebody's life. Day after day this is getting harder and harder, so they give orders that everybody should start keeping his own files as I do. If you've been allowed to exist, then it should be known how you exist. Who can remember everything they do, and especially what they *do not do*? I hope this won't sound as if I'm advocating death as a solution. No! Far from that. I'm terrified of death. I think I already mentioned this. I'm writing about disappearing just because I'm afraid of it and because I hope (like I hope I will meet Luna again) that this disappearance could miraculously disappear. Why do I write then? I write because this life, to which I'm desperately clinging, is boring, is filled with disgust, with narrow-mindedness and *fear of death.* I'm trying to fight this. Inside life, there is no solution. No, there isn't, and there's nothing that can be done about it."

***

Hrrrr-hhhhhhh, hrrrrr-hhhhhhh!

My sister is sleeping.

The mole on her cheek is slowly and slowly and slowly turning into melanosarcoma . . .

★★★

Well, sleep you bitch, sleep!

★★★

Strictly confidential.

To the Heads of the Departments of Neuropsychiatry.

Dear Sirs,

I am taking the liberty, as a complete amateur, to say a few words about you and your profession. Frankly speaking, I think that you do not know a thing about what you are doing; I mean this in relation to the soul. I am convinced that the majority of you think that the soul does not exist. I do not want to start speculating whether the soul exists or not, but even if it does not exist, you have to take the soul into consideration. You are not doing this. You only treat illnesses, i.e., whatever is manifested on the outside. In other words you force (with chemistry, whatever) certain kinds of people to behave like most people behave.

I am deeply convinced that the majority of people are never right. The fact that 99% of people slavishly follow the rules, wear the same clothes, act or do things according to certain norms, is not a proof that this is normal. If this is normal we would not have deviations which you call schizophrenia, psychosis, or neurosis.

In all likelihood, I will go mad pretty soon and wind up in one of your departments. Please bear in mind my opinion about all the things that you are going to do to me.

Respectfully.
F. B.

***

I don't know how to interpret this. I got a letter this morning. I rarely get letters. I know they don't bring anything good. The small number of letters that I receive are all official letters, in blue, cheap envelopes. In other words, letters that torment me. This one is different. It is in a pink envelope. Highly suspicious. I tore up the envelope and took out the transparent sheet of paper on which was:

I don't know what to think of all this. There is no doubt that the news is bad. So bad that I don't know how awful it is. A warning of the misfortunes ahead? Maybe! Misfortunes, only misfortunes. What else could I hope for?

★★★

"I haven't seen you in a long time," the pathologist said. "What has happened now?" There are new corpses on the table. All these people were alive when I was here last time. Now they're dead. I said that nothing special has happened to me except that I got a letter in Chinese. "In Chinese, you say." In Chinese. "You know what?" my friend said taking off his rubber gloves. "Perhaps it might be a good idea to talk to a psychiatrist."

★★★

The psychiatrist looked at me suspiciously.

– How do you feel? he asked.

– Well, you know. Sometimes it seems to me that everything around me is made up. *Staged*, if you know what I mean.

– Yes, yes.

Then he showed me a sheet of paper with an ink stain on it.

– What do you see here?

– I see an ink stain. I think you should buy a new fountain pen.

– Do you hear voices?

– Yes, of course I hear them.

– What kind?

– Voices of different people, your voice, shouting on the street.

– Do you have any other problems?

– I think I have. Recently I got a letter. A very strange letter.

– And what did this letter say?

I said:

CHI ANG CHING

– But I'm not quite sure that I have conveyed the contents of the letter accurately.

– You know what, there is nothing wrong with you. For the most part, everything is fine. Just a slight disturbance of your central nervous system. You need some rest and that's all.

I immediately felt more confident. I managed to deceive him. I managed to keep silent about the fact that I saw a face eaten up by the tumor in the ink stain and that from far away I heard the warning: "Be careful, Fritz! Be careful! They want to deceive you!" I had an advantage over the psychiatrist. I saw what he couldn't see and heard what he couldn't hear, but looking from an *angular* point of view I knew that at the same time all these things were an ink stain and the noises and what not, and I didn't want to admit what was really going on.

***

On my way out, Sigmund Freud (from the picture above the psychiatrist's head) yelled at me: *you lousy liar!* and spat at my face.

(The psychiatrist of course neither heard nor saw this.)

***

Now I'm wondering if I had gone to the hospital just because I wanted to talk to the psychiatrist and liven up the monotony of these notes with some dialogue. I didn't manage to figure out why I went there. Feeling relatively relaxed, I lay down on the bed, without taking my coat off, and decided to read. I read backwards the whole of *Don Quixote* because this seemed a more human way of reading this book. First Don Quixote dies, and then Sancho Panza's adventures follow, and then people in the book read the chapters that are coming, then Alonso Quijano is preparing for his heroic deeds and only at the very end he is reading the dusty books that inspired him to perform heroic deeds for which he died a long time ago. And that's how I discovered history is turned upside down, the true revelation that salvation lies in the past.

***

And finally: standing face to face with the past. I remember even the smallest detail of my first day in school: a crowd of short-haired, small human creatures packed in the schoolyard, under the strict surveillance of the teachers, and standing in this crowd is myself—even more short-haired and more packed in, waiting for the first class, which disgusted me from the start, because I instinctively knew that nothing good could be learned there. I saw a similar sight later on in a movie about Auschwitz: a multitude of short-haired human creatures standing packed in a kind of yard surrounded with barbed wire. The similarity couldn't be overlooked, and the purpose was similar: killing. School is a concentration camp of the soul. Its purpose is killing the innate, modest *I*, and the creation of the new *I* which would be more efficient at doing senseless jobs, *I* which is ready, if necessary, to lie in muddy ditches and patiently wait for the death of the same *I*. If you have a problem with this school-version of *I*, there is nothing that can be done about it. The number of those who have a problem with it is negligible. A human being is a durable object. It's capable of getting used to almost anything, even to this inhuman *I*, just to be able to live and be persecuted. What the elderly, those who already got used to the discomfort of this *I*, are passing on to their descendants is the view that supposedly it is good to live, and they force them to stay away from sharp objects, matches, poisonous liquids, open windows, climbing trees, touching genitalia (which they often touch), and uttering obscene words (which they never stop using). That's how you create cowards, people capable of doing anything just to save their lives, which they already lost when they were born. My first encounter with death took place in the second grade of elementary school. A friend of mine (I don't remember her name anymore because she had her name for too short a time) died in the late fall. There was something growing in her head. In her brain. This is the only thing I remember. She died during the surgery. Never again did she come to school. All right. She died, I thought, but why doesn't she come to school? Back then death didn't seem like enough of a reason to be absent from school. I envied her a little. I was having an awful time in school. Even now I'm quite convinced that it is completely unnatural for human beings, for beings in general, to sit still, straight, with their hands behind their backs. I wouldn't call this discipline at all. This procedure should be called breaking the spirit. But, I had an excellent counter-device: I yelled inside myself. As loud as I could. These yells were able to muffle the noise of whatever was going on around me. One *I* was sitting calmly and looking at the teacher respectfully, and the other *I* was fidgeting around, yelling and making faces. I have to admit that this was hypocritical. If the teacher asked me: "Aladin, what is 7x7," I would give a straight answer: "7x7=49," but deep inside me I didn't believe this. I don't believe this even today. I can, moreover, prove that 1+1 doesn't make 2. Usually we say that 1+1=2. When we say that we think of abstract units. If we replace the figures with concrete examples, with, let's say, two stones, we can say that we have two stones but we say this because we want to emphasize the fact that these two stones are standing next to one another, and not because we want to senselessly claim that these stones are "two." This is perfect nonsense. Or this old math problem (it's good that I remembered it) that I have to solve:

If a traveler goes from place A to place B, and if the distance between A and B is 86 km, and if he walks 5 km/h on average, how long will it take the traveler to get from place A to place B?

How cruel! Such unscrupulousness goes hand in hand with mathematics. Or school, in general. The problem is completely unsolvable. These clever people should know this. People who compose these kinds of problems aren't interested at all in whether or not the traveler has any reason to go from place A to place B; they simply send him or her on a trip and they blame it on the curriculum. It never even occurs to them that if anybody writes down: "If a traveler goes from place A to place B . . ." some traveler has to go from place A to place B, because that's the only way possible to make this work. Furthermore, they're not interested at all in the dangers that lurk for the traveler on that journey. It doesn't even occur to them that it might rain, in which case the traveler has to hide under some tree which brings the risk of his being killed by lightning. They just know that a traveler *has to* get in a certain number of hours to a certain place and this is where their problem ends. There is another problem that also remains a mystery to me:

How can you divide an apple into three pieces so that the first piece is double the size of the second and a third less than the third piece?

Whenever I'd encounter such a problem in real life, I'd rather give up my portion of the apple. It's better to give up your portion of the apple than to get exposed to the risk of having your *I* split in such a way that the first part is double the size of the second, and a third less than the third part. My *I* is small anyway. Italicizing does not mean that I want to emphasize and enlarge it somehow. It's a truly psychological moment. A pretty unconvincing method, I have to admit. The *I* knows best how much emphasis I put on it. What it knows—that's what it is. I think this is how it works. And if it works, it works forever. Uh, this school! So much time has passed, and I'm still paying such close attention—in writing about it—to the punctuation, introduction, exposition and conclusion. If there was anything good about school, it was the time after school. After the UNBEARABLE, *the unbearable* looked wonderful. Now it is only and exclusively *unbearable* and that's what's killing me. The monotony. It feels like time isn't passing. To compose a few sentences you need days. It hasn't always been this way, but I don't remember the time when it wasn't this way. Time slowed down with every second. Mom wanted me to be a doctor or at least an engineer. No matter how much I wanted to fulfill her wish (if only because of the spanking I would receive), I couldn't. I hardly managed to be *I* and to somehow finish a few grades in school. I want to say that it wasn't easy for me to become a nobody, somebody in front of whose name there was no space for the titles *Dr.* or *Eng.*, an *I* that I finally rejected with disgust as too big and substituted it with the bearable name Fritz.

IX

– Well, Mom, the end is near.

– The end! Already! It's not possible. What end?

– Calm down. It's just the end of my statement.

– Thank God! What will happen after?

– I don't know. It's not the end yet. It's just getting near.

***

Maya was the only one who was left, the daughter of Judge Ivanović. They lived on the first floor of our building. Judge Ivanović went out very rarely, while the mother never went out. Perhaps they didn't have a mother. Even today, you can find the words MAYA CRAZY engraved on the stairwell. I engraved them with a pocketknife one evening when the stairwell was empty.

Maya looked almost like what was on the drawing. What she really looked like—I forget. A lot of time has passed since then. I remember that she had a nice mole on her cheek and I found it very attractive. One day my NKVD doubt admitted: "You are in love with Maya." This caused me a lot of trouble. It wasn't easy loving somebody and hating yourself at the same time. But what could I do? Nothing! At that time I called myself Maya too. The way I call myself Fritz now. A little more and I would have completely identified myself with Maya and thus stopped hating MYSELF, because I was becoming somebody else, a more beautiful *I*, because this overweight *I* was turning into a nice-smelling and soft SHE! But one night, drawn by a reddish light oozing through the window of Maya's room, I climbed on the sill and peeped inside. Maya was lying on a huge bed completely naked, her legs slightly raised and spread . . .

***

"My God, My God" my mom will say when she secretly reads these lines. "And I thought Maya was a good girl."

***

A whole regiment of lead soldiers ready for combat was standing in a perfect line on the nightstand. Maya was taking them one by one and putting them between her legs . . .

***

Judge Ivanović throws open the door with a bang and jumps into the room. Maya hides herself under the covers. Through the glass I can't hear what he's saying. I just see the movement of his lips. But, we know very well what he's saying. Then he takes the "Criminal Law" book from the shelf, puts it on the table and starts lining up the soldiers in a combat line. The hearings don't take long. The verdict is always the same: death. After the trial, Judge Ivanović takes a sharp knife and chops off the soldiers' heads one by one.

***

"Who would have thought this?" my mom would say. "Such a nice gentleman. Such a well-mannered gentleman."

***

I jump off the sill, run back home, close myself in my room, lie on a bed; I take a pillow, comforter, blankets, old newspapers, pieces of clothes, the lamp, books and hug them all as hard as I can in order to deserve to exist in this, at least for a little bit, at least in this way.

***

I start hating myself even more. I hate Maya too. But still I love her. The mole on her cheek was greater than my hate. Luckily, not long after that, Maya ran away with the piano teacher. Judge Ivanović died. They took him to the autopsy room to my friend's predecessor. They buried him afterwards. By now he must be a big boy. Somewhere in the vicinity. I'm sure he's collecting lead soldiers.

***

"Sure," my mom will say glowingly. "Anybody could have guessed that she ran away with that bum. Poor Judge Ivanović."

***

I'm not sure I told the whole truth about Maya. My NKVD doubt is accusing me of faking everything. That I left out some important facts. First, it says that her name was not Maya. This is the result of a sick imagination. "Don't fool yourself," my NKVD doubt is telling me cynically. "You know very well that her name was Chiang Ching. She was Chinese. And you were Chinese. And her father was Chinese. We were all Chinese." All right, but these claims are contradicting the unquestionable fact that *now* I'm not Chinese and that I'm a thousand kilometers away from China. "But, what's now is now," my doubt says. "The past has no boundaries. There is nothing impossible. Didn't you write yourself a letter about that?" Did I? Perhaps.

Chiang Ching had an enchanting mole on her cheek. Somehow I loved her. On the dirty wall of our building I engraved with a pocketknife a couple of unpleasant things about her. This is my self-critique. Last time when I was in this building everything was the way I left it. You could read on the wall:

My fascination with bourgeois habits (Chiang Ching was to blame for this) caused me a lot of trouble. In the period of reconstruction there's no room for love. Still, I admit I loved her. A little more and I would have lost my head and abandoned myself completely to the petty-bourgeois impulse of love. But! (Always this *but*, this vile word used by defeatists, skeptics and revisionists), but one evening I did something that at first glance seemed to be utterly indecent, which was proof that I was under the great influence of bourgeois habits and morals. Going back home, I was tempted to peep into her room through the slit between the window and the curtain. My intentions were honorable. I wanted to see Chiang Ching without being noticed. What I saw threw me into despair: Chiang Ching was sitting on her bed and arranging the I Ching sticks. I ran to my room and was depressed the entire night. Before dawn I went out in the hallway and engraved on the wall the following words with my pocket knife:

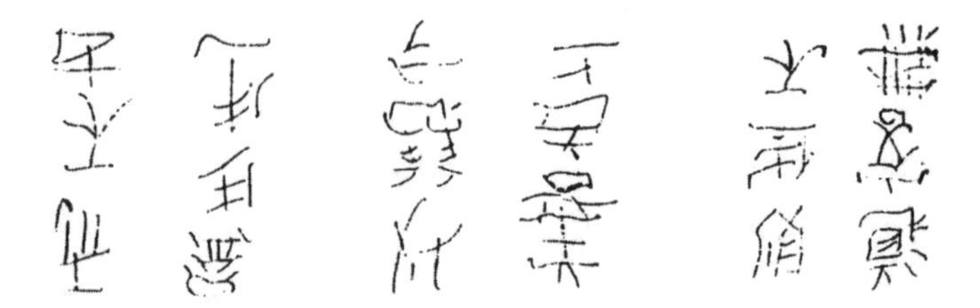

Chiang Ching was soon discovered. For a long time I didn't hear anything about her. I was pretending that this didn't interest me. Later on I found out that she disappeared in one of the Cultural Revolution purges. That's all about this topic.

***

"Forget about that now," my mom says. "Your sister wants to make up with her husband. His father is here too."

***

Wonderful!

***

Sister: I know, I made lots of mistakes. I didn't know how to appreciate your kindness. I'm sorry. I'll never do it again.

Mongoloid: No, no! It's my fault. I wasn't careful enough. I'm sorry. I'll never do it again.

Mom: The most important thing is that you two make up.

Mongoloid's father: Yes, yes, when the children are born

everything will be different.

(Like hell it will be different. Everything will stay just the same. Even worse. And now children. This will just multiply their misfortunes.)

I: Of course, children will be the solution to all problems.

(Everybody cries.)

Mongoloid's father: Allow me to please read you one of my poems.

(From his inside pocket he takes out a piece of paper.)

"It has been raining for days. Through the window of her room she was looking at the city.

Fish were looking back at her from the other side."

(Everybody applauds.)

★★★

– Will you really finish soon? my mother asks.

– I will. The sooner the better. I already feel sick of all this.

– What a pity! Just when it was getting interesting.

★★★

I'm sitting and watching my mom, the mongoloid, my sister and the butcher. I'm sitting and watching the room in which we're sitting: the pictures on the walls, the rugs, and the lights on the ceiling. I'm sitting and more and more I feel disgusted by everything. I'm sitting and thinking about what I should do.

Suddenly I take all these things and tear them up into small pieces. I burn the remnants in the ashtray, open the window and throw out the ashes.

***

"Fritz!" My mom is furious. "How many times did I tell you not to empty ashtrays through the window?"

***

And again the letter. Blue. Not registered:

There is no use beating around the bush, I have to tell you immediately: you are not you. You did not have a memory when you were replaced. You did not notice anything; you would never have noticed if I had not told you this. You will probably be mad at me because I told you this, but my intentions are good. The fact that you are not you is not so important in this life, but in death—this is important. In this endless loneliness, in this endless big and small, everything is only what it really is. I hope you understand this. It's much better for you to reconcile yourself with this while you are still alive because—no matter how painful this may be—you are still somebody, you are not nobody, true, you are somebody who does not know anything about himself because he thinks he is somebody else. Your whole life you have been a stranger, you have been wearing this stranger like you are wearing somebody else's suit; this suit is not there anymore, you are stark naked, and your pulse is going up to 170. Soon your sister who is not your sister anymore will come into your room and say: "Fritz, you got a letter. Is it bad news?" You will make up something. You will be standing by the window, not daring to look at her, and you won't know what to think of all this because—yes, you got a letter, but I am not your enemy, I am a friend of somebody who is not you. You do not know me at all. How can I be your friend? Our friendship referred to something else, to something that nobody (not even you or me) could understand. You will think: "This is one of their jokes." I leave this possibility open. The possibilities are endless, but the worst one always happens. Nothing can be changed here.

Think about it for a while.

***

A little bit after this, my sister comes in. "Fritz, I see that you got a letter. You seem worried. Is it bad news?"

"No . . . It's a letter from an old friend."

***

I'm standing by the window and I don't know what to think.

***

I want to hear . . .

X

It looks like I was going back to some place. It must have been during the night because the streetlamps were on, the few that were still unbroken; of course, only the unbroken ones would be on. I must have been walking by the river: keeping pace with me there was black water flowing by and I thought that I would get too tired to keep pace with the water, but I still continued walking to prove that it's impossible for a traveler to walk the distance between some place A and some place B. There was no doubt (at least not for me) that this was impossible. True, I started from some place A, but this place for me was *here*, I was standing in this place, then I started walking and thinking I'd get to some place after all, but I had time to convince myself that I got nowhere, that I actually didn't move. I was always *here*. Wherever I would stop, I was *here*, I couldn't move a centimeter out of this *here*, I couldn't get rid of the adverbial nightmare *here*. I was walking, my steps were disappearing in the past tense. When I reached the park (the same park in which I couldn't find the way out of the hopeless sentences), I parted ways with the river. The river continued further, and I turned left or right. I was a little bit sorry I parted ways with the river. All partings are equally sad. But, I'll come back one day to this river, no doubt about that, I'll come back to her for good. That's why there are bridges. The street was going straight, and on each side of it the side streets branched out, full of shadows of unspecified objects and that's where I wanted to go because they led nowhere; especially if you're walking around aimlessly, like I did, they led you nowhere. The shadow of a girl carrying a ball crossed the street. The girl herself couldn't be seen. I don't blame her. She had to be in bed by eight, and this eight could have even been twenty years ago. I followed the shadow, quietly, on my toes, staying very close to the walls of the building, just as in Agatha Christie novels. I followed the shadow for about a hundred meters, and then the shadow of the girl stopped and looked at the shadow of a bell tower. A little bit after that, a shadow of a boy appeared. They started walking together holding hands. I followed them, very quietly, just as in Agatha Christie novels. What a coincidence! The shadows went into a hallway of the building where I lived. From the street I saw them going down to the basement. It made no sense to spy on them further. The basement was completely dark and you couldn't see the shadows. Now I was completely convinced that no traveler can ever make it from place A to place B. I guess I wanted to prove this. I walked into my room, sat on the edge of the bed and covered my face with my hands. I was *I*, I was *now*, I was *here*. There was nothing I could do for myself. Time and place were holding me in a tight grip.

***

That day I bought 200 aspirin. Aspirin is good for all kinds of things. At first I swallowed three or four of them. They were a bit sour. Their taste gave me an idea about which I will expound later. I immediately felt better. I mean physically. A heap of papers was sitting on the table. This reminded me that I should be writing. The beneficial effect of the aspirin suddenly wore off. It occurred to me that I could tear up everything into small pieces, burn them in an ashtray and throw the ashes out the window. I could easily have done this. My mom was sleeping. But I had to write. It made no sense to destroy everything at the very end. They would no doubt come again. The worst thing that could happen to me would be I'd have to rewrite the whole thing word for word. I couldn't bear this. I took ten more aspirin so that I wouldn't die. I was still sad. But at least I wasn't dead. I was sad because I knew that somewhere around here, relatively close to me, was SHE (Luna), and that I, most probably, would never see her again. It has never happened to me that I twice see a person I really care about. But, to make all this more absurd, I wasn't losing hope that I'd see HER despite everything. Hope is a serious illness. I took a couple more aspirin. Aspirin can cure everything. Understandably, my head became heavy.

That's why I took a couple more aspirin. I felt like an animal caught in a trap. I made an attempt to cry. It wasn't working. The phrase *an animal caught in a trap* is not a figure of speech. I felt just like an animal, and my room with all the objects in it, felt like a trap. It's not a figure of speech. I was really caught in a trap, who knows for how long I'd been trapped, but I realized it only then. I couldn't move anywhere from my trap. All right: this shouldn't be taken literally. Nobody was stopping me from going out into the street, walking to the pharmacy and buying, let's say, 200 more aspirin, but what about after that? I would have to return to this room because my place is *here*. I don't like this place, but I belong here. I already said this: I was caught in its trap. And here I was, left not to hunters, but to myself. I swallowed two more aspirin. Just in order to interrupt this disturbing stream of thought.

★★★

I wanted to hear "Fascination."

I turned on the radio.

It was late.

I turned off the radio.

It got even later.

I started whistling "Fascination."

The neighbor started banging on the wall: tap, tap, tap, tap.

This woke up another neighbor. He got up, took a saxophone and started playing.

From the floor above came the sounds of the piano.

The neighbor from the building across the street opened the window and started strumming on a guitar.

The bassist somehow appeared in the street.

I took my accordion harmonica.

My sister woke up and yelled: "O yeah!"

My mom went out in her pajamas, listened to the jazz and started singing:

"Nobody knows the trouble . . . "

It was crazy.

Aspirin is the real thing.

I always claimed this.

But morning! The letters come in the morning. Blue, registered, official:

We are coming today. Your manuscript should be ready.

Illegible seal
Illegible signatures

***

I counted pages. Only *eighty-six.*

They said—about hundred.

This can mean eighty, but also one hundred and twenty.

Given all the possibilities (I already said this)

The worst one is the most likely . . .

It means there should be a hundred and twenty pages.

Where can I find about forty pages?

★★★

"Where can I find forty pages of text?" I asked my friend the pathologist. He was preparing somebody's liver and whistling "Fascination." I hope I need not mention that the corpses of the people who were quite alive during my last visit to the autopsy room were lying on the tables.

★★★

"I don't know, I really don't know," the pathologist said. "I'm pretty sure you can't find them here. You wrote everything you had to say about the autopsy room."

★★★

One corpse looked familiar for some reason. I stooped to get a better look. It was Maya, the daughter of Judge Ivanović. I recognized her by the mole on her upper lip.

★★★

– What did she die of? I asked.

– Angina pectoris!

★★★

I had coffee there and was getting ready to leave.

– What's with your mom? my friend wanted to know.

– She's fine. They brought her back home.

– All's well when it's over.

***

He had nothing more to say to me. I mean, he didn't have anything to say that I should write down, nothing that I could put in my statement.

***

I ran away. Even while I was writing the first lines, I knew I wasn't going to finish my statement. What seemed to be the smartest thing for me to do was to go somewhere. I walked the whole night. Why would I be waiting for the two guys? They probably came yesterday and asked for me. I'm tired, but I keep going. My persecutors are probably at my heels.

***

I'll refrain from making an assumption that I went crazy in the negative sense of this word and I'll write a few lines about nature. And about the birds. About the birds especially. The landscape is beautiful. The place is swarming with birds and they all chirp "Fascination." The place is swarming with birds. A multitude of all kinds of birds but I don't know what any of them are called. They (the birds) aren't bothered by that at all. They aren't interested in names, they don't care about me, they don't even notice me, except perhaps as a possible threat. I feel terribly inferior to birds. Because I have reason. I can't fly because I have reason. To be able to fly you can't have reason and the logic that is constantly nagging at you that it's *impossible* to fly. A human being, supposedly, isn't able to fly because of his anatomy. Bullshit! We lost our wings because we tried to understand the mechanics of flying. That's why we are on Earth. But we aren't free. We are chained to the Earth.

***

Then water. Water is making me think. There is a stream nearby. I spent the whole morning sitting by that stream. I'm made of water. It took me forty years to realize this. True, I'm not entirely made of water, but *the thing that* I *call I* is diluted in 36° C water. That's how things are: I'm a chemical solution. And why, then, if I'm made of water can't I walk on water? There is nothing to convince me that this isn't possible. Of course, I didn't try to step on the ruffled surface of the stream. My logic is functioning perfectly, and according to its criteria this is impossible.

***

Logic: You idiot, you're heavier than water, and all bodies heavier than water sink and at the same time they displace the amount of liquid they themselves weigh, just as the Archimedes principle teaches us. I (understandably) accept this. But there is something, and fortunately I don't know what that is, that opposes this logic and this slavish adherence to the laws of heavenly mechanics, of connected tubes: the law of inertia.

I: What do you mean *heavier*? That's being prejudiced. I'm heavier than a certain amount of water, but when compared to the whole mass of the sea, I'm even more negligible than a feather.

Logic: Well, why don't you step on it?

I: I'm afraid.

Logic: You see, I'm right.

I: No. You aren't.

***

Unfortunately, I don't dare step onto the surface of the stream. Not because I couldn't do that, but because I don't deserve to do so. Only those who are more perfect than water can stay on the surface of it, and I hardly deserve even to be walking on the ground. Besides, the water in the stream is so clean and clear. And *I*? I'm nontransparent. Murky, nontransparent, lost.

***

During the night I made my own plan for the salvation of humankind. The plan is basically simple: *retreat into yourself.* Nothing else. Cut off all dealings with the world. I hope my plan will be looked at kindly. In my enthusiasm, I'm almost positive about that. But, to be able to realize this plan, certain things have to be changed about people. I'm not sure how this might work.

***

First (and the most important) thing: With blisteringly hot needles, poke out everybody's eyes and thus get rid of terrifying visual contact.

Second: Cut out everybody's tongues and thus get rid of the nightmare of speech.

Third: Before these other measures, everyone should be castrated or sterilized.

This would be all.

Simple, isn't it?

***

True, this would hurt, but a little pain and discomfort (which we know is necessary for the realization of all big ideas) will bring magnificent rewards. All of the illusions will disappear forever. The silence and our concentration on the only thing left—ourselves—will transform the whole universe. All eternity will luxuriate in its glory, and in its darkness the bluish sparks of all the numberless *I*'s, all the *I*'s that ever existed, will be glimmering. And each and every *I* will need only its own light. There won't be any further misunderstanding between individual *I*'s, because it will be clear all *I*'s are one and the same thing. And that will be the end of all confusion, the end of death, because then even disappearance will disappear. And when disappearance disappears—what can disappear? Nothing. Because there never was anything except my vision, and the whole nightmare of existence is just a perfidious conspiracy of my senses. Something like a horror movie.

XI

I got back to town early this morning. It was clear to me that there was nothing to be afraid of. Besides, I was approaching the 100th page of my statement. That's quite a lot. Word by word, sentence by sentence and there you get a mess. I wanted to go to the Academy of Sciences and present to the scholars my perspective on death and my idea of salvation. Since my enthusiasm wore off a little bit, I didn't dare enter the building of the Academy. I was pacing up and down in front of the entrance and dared to walk in just about noon. I wanted to pass unnoticed by the doorman but he didn't pay any attention to me anyway. He was doing a crossword puzzle. Just when I was about to step onto the stairwell, I felt dizzy. I had just enough strength to lower myself onto the pile of old paper and cardboard boxes below the stairwell. I knew that I couldn't reach the top floors of the Academy. Then, completely worn out, I fell asleep.

***

I woke up in the city dump. This was to be expected. I was lying on a heap of paper under the stairwell for quite a long time. The pile of paper under the Academy stairwell certainly couldn't stay there forever. Somebody didn't like this—all this mess—and they ordered that it be cleaned up. And—here I am on the dump, the city dump, together with other useless things. But I'm not complaining. I've come to terms with the situation. To be discarded on the dump, even by mistake, is nothing when compared to what can happen to people. I was sitting rather comfortably—the ground of the dump is soft—and I was looking at the sky. There is nothing symbolic in this. I simply found myself in such a position—my face turned towards the sky. I'm lying on my back and I'm writing the last lines. I'm not thinking about anything specific. I don't feel bitter for not having had a chance to present to the scholars my vision of the salvation of the world.

***

"You have disgraced our family forever," my mom tells me. Somebody saw me lying on the dump, and told somebody else, and that person told somebody else, and that's how my mom found out that I was thrown on the dump.

***

"The two guys came looking for you last night," my sister says. Her belly is big and round. Soon she'll have a baby. I feel sorry for this creature.

***

"Fritz, why don't you come back home? Everything will be all right," my brother-in-law tells me. The son of the butcher across the street.

***

What shall I tell them?

***

I might have even come up with the answer to this question if the two of them didn't appear. They stopped a few hundred yards from us and were silently observing what was going on.

***

That same moment my mom, my sister, and my brother-in-law turned into a mist that got blown away by the wind.

***

– Salajdin Bejs, alias Fritz, we're here.

– I see.

– Yesterday you weren't at home.

– I wasn't.

– You wanted to run away?

(I don't know what I should say.)

"No, I wanted to gain time to finish my report," my prompter whispers to me.

– No, I didn't want to run away. I wanted to gain some time to finish the statement.

– But, you should have waited for us. We've already put in a report that you ran away. This won't be a very good thing for you.

(More pathos, more pathos! the director is yelling.)

– All right. I'll accept responsibility. Anyway, your deadline was *soon*, and this is pretty unspecific, isn't it?

– Do you think it would have been better if we gave you a more specific deadline?

– I think this would have been much better.

– You see, I don't think so. You're not taking your work seriously. Instead of writing what you have in a couple of days, you were wandering around the city and wasting your time doing some stupid things.

– Writing isn't an easy job.

– We didn't request very much. They told us about a hundred pages, we told you this and that's it. Nobody said anything about what kind of hundred pages. You should just have written them; there was no need to worry about the style. How far did you get?

– About 94 pages.

– Only?

(Be rougher! the director is shouting.)

– Only? he said and kicked me in the side with his leg. Three months for just 94 pages!

– I had nothing more to say.

– All right. Give us the manuscript.

***

There you see, I was thinking while the two of them were reading the manuscript, soon enough all this will come to an end and I'll be free. I'll break my Remington typewriter, break the pencils, tear up the paper and will never write again. *She* said we would see each other as soon as I was done with my writing. I might even see her tonight. I'll go to the stuffy bar and order a beer. And wait for her to come. She will come. Didn't she say she always keeps her word?

***

I have been dead for months now, Moira writes. *Even after my death I haven't stopped thinking about you. I have plenty of time. I look at my father who is visiting my grave. I am nowhere. Sometimes I glance down there and with some satisfaction I see that the lips that you kissed are turning into a gooey substance full of white worms, and the eyes (at which you never dared to look) are becoming dry mucus.*

Moira

***

This letter doesn't exist. How did these pink letters end up on the dump? But this is only making the situation worse. I can't burn it, tear it or lose it.

Why doesn't it keep quiet?

***

– Well Fritz, we read your statement.

– And what now?

– Now, we are going to have a little talk.

– About what?

– We ask the questions here.

– Well ask then. I want this to end.

– Me too, the tall one says. I'm trying to make it to the dog races.

– Me too, his friend says. It's my son's birthday today.

– Who is Moira?

– She's the daughter of our neighbor. The one I wanted to strangle. I hope you read this.

– Impossible! I checked this! The neighbor really exists, you got into a fight with him because of the noise, but he doesn't have a daughter.

– Not anymore. She died.

– Fritz, don't lie. Your neighbor has never had a daughter.

– I'm sure he has one. Actually, that he *had* one.

– Listen, you should have written a statement. You understand? You should have written what you had been doing, but you wrote a kind of novel. Sort of. We don't come from the Institute of Literature. We want facts.

("Cry. You should cry here," the prompter says.)

I pretend to be crying. I must be doing this convincingly because my persecutors are grinning and nudging each other.

– Fritz, Fritz! Crying won't help you.

– I know.

– So, why are you crying?

– I'm hungry.

– That's the only reason?

– That's the only reason. I fainted from hunger on the stairwell of the Academy of Sciences.

– Yes, we've been informed about that. You wanted to save the world.

– No! I wanted all this to end as soon as possible.

– Why?

– Because it's getting boring.

– And? What else?

– To be able to see a beautiful girl again that I met in the bar. She promised to see me when all this is over.

Suddenly my persecutors start roaring with laughter. I don't understand what's so funny.

– He's thinking of Natasha.

– Yes, yes, he probably is thinking of Natasha.

– Who's Natasha?

– The girl you met.

– How do you know this?

– We sent her. We thought you'd finish sooner if you believed that you'd see her once again.

– I won't see her ever again?

– Will he see her? the tall guy asks his pal. The silent persecutor shakes his head.

– You won't see her again. It's not in the plan that you should see her again.

– Well then, all this makes no sense.

– That's not our problem. Goodbye, Fritz!

– Goodbye.

***

I come home and I see my mother crying. I don't dare ask her why she's crying. As if she didn't have enough reasons for that: Her husband is dead, her daughter is getting married and getting divorced, she's snatched by the white slave merchants, and her son is thrown on the city dump like a dead dog.

A really sad old age.

***

At the end just a couple of words Mom a couple of sentences before we fall asleep I hope for the last time before some other awakening it was a long time ago Mom I wanted to say something and I couldn't I don't remember anymore what I wanted to say what I could have said what I'm saying anyway I don't even know what I'm writing and I'm trying to remember but it's not working Mom I wrote everything I said everything I remained empty like the empty shell of a sea snail if such snails exist and what I said doesn't exist has never ever existed even if I could speak I wouldn't be able to say this Mom the sentences are so strange fluttery casual they don't make you do anything and I wish this could last that my brain remain washed out with no Morse codes inside with no wishes no hope Mom my Mom such strange sentences are appearing about the stains that turn into a human shape my own human shape on the wall across the table and because of this I start suspecting start doubting myself start accusing myself that I'm spying on myself it's impossible to distinguish all these sentences because there are no commas no periods no exclamation marks it seems these aren't sentences after all but only words that stand in a certain relationship to one another and any meaning here is just pure coincidence no and no there is no sense here how could this make any sense this is just a story if it is a story if it's not I'm still here this is made of lead but they were sick and whho are they and swhat are they I don't knorrr and they andthey nor they when they read this it will be five in the afternoon rain will fall they will think: look, how could he know it was 17.00? Just for a moment there are punctuation marks because they will say this but they are no longer here I won't be here there won't be a table there I won't be sitting at a table on the wall across from the table there won't be the stain there won't be anything I'll be walking and breathing I just hope my slant eyes will my face will my hands will do something and I'll be waiting for somebody to figure out the game to wake up to call me on the phone I'll be waiting waiting and wait again no matter what this I'm saying is saying you should not pay attention to this this is just a story nothing else this is what the persons in charge said nothing dif-fer-ent could have happened they read my story long ago thought about it for a long time about it . . .

***

"You put it so nicely," my mom says.

***

– Mom!

– Yes, my son.

– She was so beautiful.

– Who?

– I don't know.

***

And my mom falls asleep.

***

I take the typewriter and tiptoe to the attic. I type three times (quietly): knock, knock, knock . . . Nobody answers. I go in and find the awful sight. Somebody gouged out the eyes of the *mechanical woman*, broke both her hands, broke her ribs and pierced her Singer heart with a long steel rod . . .

***

SIT REQUIESCAT IN PACE

***

Somewhat later a phone rang.

"What are you doing?" my pathologist friend asks. He was sad.

"Nothing special. I'm trying to finish up my novel."

"Have you found forty pages?"

"No. It didn't work out."

"Fritz . . ." my friend the pathologist said and fell silent. The receiver emitted only the ominous crackling of electricity. You'd have to be an electronical engineer it this to make sense.

"Yes."

"Fritz, do you know that some of those who'll be lying on the autopsy room tables tomorrow are still alive?"

"I know."

"I wish you a good night, Fritz."

"Pi-pii, pi-pii, pi-pii," the telephone said. Dimitrije Statute 1111—CHINESE LETTER

"Woof, woof, woof," the walls spoke.

***

I looked out the window. It was raining. As far as I could see down the street, there was one dead Fritz dangling from each of the lampposts.

***

Nice view indeed.

***

I wanted to hear "Fascination."

I turned on the radio.

The news was on.

"Raymond Queneau died."

I turned off the radio.

But Raymond Queneau was still dead.